THE RELUCTANT BRIDE

Christine is forced into marriage with Adam Kyle, a wealthy and handsome entrepreneur whom she despises, in order to save her late father's reputation. At first Christine wants nothing to do with him; she tells him she hates everything he stands for. But during their honeymoon in the Friendly Islands her opinion of him changes, and she realises that she has misjudged him. Now she no longer feels embittered, true love blossoms among the sheltering palms.

Books by Dorothy Purdy
in the Linford Romance Library:

CONFLICT OF TRUST
BITTER LEGACY

DOROTHY PURDY

THE RELUCTANT BRIDE

Complete and Unabridged

LINFORD
Leicester

First published in Great Britain in 2005

First Linford Edition
published 2006

British Library CIP Data

Purdy, Dorothy
    The reluctant bride.—Large print ed.—
Linford romance library
    1. Love stories
    2. Large type books
    I. Title
    823.9′2 [F]

    ISBN 1–84617–452–X

Published by
F. A. Thorpe (Publishing)
Anstey, Leicestershire

Set by Words & Graphics Ltd.
Anstey, Leicestershire
Printed and bound in Great Britain by
T. J. International Ltd., Padstow, Cornwall

This book is printed on acid-free paper

1

'Marry you? I wouldn't marry you if you were the last man on earth!' Christine Bradley's blue eyes blazed defiance.

'There must be dozens of women who would be only too glad to be Mrs Adam Kyle. Why not marry one of them? Why would you want to marry me?'

Adam looked unperturbed as he sat down on the settee.

'There are several reasons. I don't intend to go into all of them.' He gave a dismissive shrug. 'For instance, after our wedding, I would rid myself of the monstrous regiment of women who view me as marriage bait. That's worth a lot for a start.'

He looked at her with a smile of satisfaction on his face like a cat that had swallowed the cream.

Not a man to be trifled with, she

recalled, was her father's description of Adam that first evening when he'd brought him back to the house. She couldn't even remember. It seemed ages ago now. But even before they'd met, she knew of his reputation as a successful entrepreneur. How could she avoid it? There was some mention of one of his companies in the financial columns nearly every week, praising the man for his business acumen, a view Christine didn't share.

'I don't know why you've invited him here,' she'd said to her father. 'The Press may call him an entrepreneur, but that's just a nice term for it. I call him an asset stripper.' Her voice was husky with fury. 'I hate everything he stands for. Making a profit is all he cares about with no thought for the workforce at all. What about all those people who lose their jobs?'

The more she thought about it, the less able she was to contain her wrath. 'He's a rip-off merchant of the worst possible kind. I don't know how the business fraternity can be taken in by him.'

But when she met him socially, as she was obliged to do on several occasions, she realised the far-reaching effects of his influence, his determination to succeed, no matter the cost. Those were the qualities his business colleagues obviously admired, but it didn't alter her opinion of him.

That he was wealthy and utterly charming there was no doubt, an intoxicating combination to most women. Unlike her, they didn't seem to realise how ruthless he was, how the surface charm was merely a façade.

'That's all very well for you,' Christine replied furiously, returning to the present. 'You're putting yourself first as usual, but it won't work, Adam,' she spat out. 'Nothing would induce me to marry you, nothing!'

Adam was undeterred, however.

'Ours wouldn't be like any other marriage,' he went on. 'The circumstances are dramatically different. After

3

what's happened, I'm afraid you haven't any choice in the matter.'

Christine could feel her heart pounding against her ribs. What was he up to?

'After what has happened? I don't know what you mean.'

'I'll begin at the beginning,' he said. 'You'd better sit down, Christine. Did you ever wonder why Jonathan Childes didn't come to your father's funeral?'

Puzzled, Christine sat down as she was bid, wondering why he'd brought up this subject. Jonathan Childes had been her father's best friend. How did he fit into the equation? She couldn't make head nor tail of his question and took her time before she replied.

'Yes, I did,' she said, trying to speak in an even tone. 'When he didn't attend, I assumed he was away on some business trip. I sent him a letter telling him father had died, but when I didn't hear from him, I thought . . . '

'I'm afraid it wasn't as simple as that. For your sake, I only wish it was,' Adam interrupted, placing his hand gently on her arm.

'This isn't going to be easy, Christine. I want you to listen to what I have to say and not interrupt until I've finished.'

Christine twisted away from him, trying to hide the shock she knew was evident in her face. What was he going to tell her now?

'You know that Jonathan did a fair amount of business with your father?'

Christine nodded.

'Well, he asked your father to place some of his most valuable antiques at Sotheby's while he was abroad,' Adam said. 'Your father had them auctioned under his own name and told Childes that would make the sale more straightforward. The antiques fetched a considerable sum, but your father told Childes that they sold for a fraction of the price they actually realised. Your father kept the rest of the proceeds for himself,' he went on. 'Childes didn't ask for a receipt because he trusted your father, but he found out afterwards how he had been duped. Your father kept the majority of the realised price in order to prop up Bradley's Fine Arts & Antiques.'

Christine felt panic rising in the pit of her stomach.

'You mean Father committed fraud?' She was very aware of her own voice, shrill and out of control. 'No, I won't have it. He couldn't. He wouldn't . . . '

'The plain fact is, he did. You can imagine Childes' reaction when he found out. At first, he wanted to go to the police and if he had, your father would most certainly have gone to jail. Fortunately, because of his previous friendship with your father, Childes was persuaded not to take any action. I made sure he signed a legal agreement stating that the matter would be kept confidential and my company paid him the realised sale price in full.'

Christine couldn't believe it. How could her father have done such a thing? Why didn't he tell her? Why did he let Adam bail him out? Her mind in turmoil, she tried to reassure herself that for some unknown reason, Adam had made it all up. It couldn't be true. There must be some mistake. He was saying all this for his own ends. Her father was honest, through and through, but when she started to protest, Adam made it clear he could verify everything he'd said.

She struggled to recover her composure, her sanity, her self-respect.

'Even if what you say can be proved,' she stammered, 'and I want clear evidence of that, I still won't marry you. I don't love you. I don't even like you. I'd never chose you for a husband, not ever. It would be . . . '

'The ultimate sacrifice? Is that what you're trying to say? Don't you understand yet? It isn't a case of you choosing me. If you don't want this thing to become common knowledge, I'm the only choice you've got. Think about it, Christine. After all that has happened, and my personal involvement, you can't look elsewhere for a partner. We're bound together.'

Blinking back the tears, she rounded on him furiously.

'It's blackmail. You can't be serious. You can't expect me to . . . '

'Believe me, Christine, I've never been more serious in my life,' he said with dangerous softness. 'Just think for a moment what you're getting out of it — a guarantee of secrecy, combined with a secure, financial future. What could be fairer than that? So it's make-your-mind-up time. Marry me, or the word's out!'

* * *

Christine hid behind the veil of fine lace which hid her face, a good thing, too, she thought grimly as she peered out from behind it, because she certainly wasn't smiling. Her brides-maids grouped themselves around her, making sure there were no creases in her dress, and that her flowered headdress stayed in place. It was such a heavy burden knowing she could never disclose the real reason she was marrying Adam, not even to her closest friends. She was living a lie. Only those immediately involved knew the truth, and they'd been sworn to secrecy. No-one else must ever know, not ever. She had too much pride for that.

The church bells stopped ringing and the first strains of the wedding march swelled out. As the congregation stood, she struggled against her feelings of deep apprehension. Her hands trembled. Her godfather, who was giving her away, stood at her side.

'Are you all right, Chris?' he asked in a worried tone.

'I'm all right,' she whispered back, and clung to his arm for support.

But she wasn't all right — far from it. How could she be all right when she was about to take part in a meaningless charade? But her god-father didn't know that. Nobody in the congregation did. It was a secret she had to keep, no matter what.

She thought her head would explode as she began her walk down the aisle. She'd agreed to this course of action against her better judgement, and she knew she was getting into deeper water with every step she took, but she knew there was no way out, unless she turned and ran, and what would be solved by doing that?

As she approached the altar steps, her stomach churned in fear and alarm. Damn you, Adam Kyle, she thought to herself, for putting me in this position.

She caught sight of him standing in the front pew, motionless, waiting. He towered over his best man, his formal dress accentuating his height and the broad span of his shoulders. She knew no woman in her right mind could deny his charismatic attraction, only she wasn't in her right mind, was she? In her right mind she would put as much distance between them as possible.

Reaching the altar steps, she handed her bouquet to her chief bridesmaid and with a tense, nervous gesture, lifted her veil. Taking a step forward in order to reach her side, Adam turned and faced her.

'You look lovely,' he murmured, his voice a smoky purr.

He was at it again, trying every angle, she thought scornfully, treating her to the full measure of his charm. Taking up his position in front of the bride and groom, the vicar smiled at them over the top of his prayer book.

When it came to the time to make her responses, Christine's voice wavered a little. Did anyone notice that tremor of uncertainty, she wondered. Adam had no such trouble with his. His voice was resonant, deep and confident, sounding for all the world as though he meant every word he said.

But I know better than that, Christine thought to herself. He knows what he's getting out of this marriage. It isn't that he cares one jot for me. It's what's in it for him that counts. He's ruthless.

'You may kiss the bride.'

The vicar's words burned in her brain. She hadn't counted on that. She didn't want him to kiss her with the vicar and the whole congregation bearing witness. She didn't want him to kiss her at all, but she knew that custom demanded it, and she braced herself as Adam took her in his arms.

He kissed her very slowly and deliberately. He was staking his claim in front of the whole congregation, and he deepened the kiss with expertise. The moment seemed endless, and when he finally released her she drew in a breath.

Her response had astounded her. What was it about this man? When they'd kissed, an electric current had shot between them which was impossible to ignore. Her bones had melted, and a ribbon of liquid fire had seared her heart. The thought of it was more than she could bear. Whatever had possessed her? Perhaps she'd never know, but of one thing she was certain. Adam Kyle was highly dangerous to her peace of mind.

'So you're no ice-maiden after all,' he

murmured softly as the vicar led the way to the vestry. 'I don't think we'll have a problem when we share a bed.'

The blood rushed to her face, but she ignored that remark, and it was with a trembling hand that she signed the register. The photographers waiting outside the church were busily shouting instructions as soon as they appeared.

'Put your arm around her waist. Go on, give her a squeeze. That's right, now give her another one. O.K, it's a wrap.'

Adam smiled and responded, talking back to them in a jocular way, all new possessiveness of his newly-acquired bride, all practised charm. Christine tried to shrug him off, but all to no avail. At last it was over. Placing his hand under her elbow, Adam guided her towards the waiting limousine.

'I can manage perfectly well, thank you,' she blurted out, shrugging him off and looping her long train over her arm. 'Just leave me alone.'

The driver, holding the car door open, gave them a brief smile.

'Get in and don't argue,' Adam muttered under his breath and she could tell by his tone that his patience was wearing thin.

Lowering herself into the back seat, she froze him with an icy look. Just because they'd gone through some pointless wedding ceremony, he needn't think she belonged to him. He'd soon find out she wouldn't always be willing to do as he said. This was the twenty-first century. She wasn't some scullery maid who had to obey her master.

Edging herself away from him, she pretended to arrange the folds of her wedding gown around her feet.

'I'm sure you've packed suitable clothes for a small Pacific island,' Adam said. 'Sarongs are the order of the day. Can't wait to see how you look in one.'

Then you'll have a long wait, Christine thought to herself, although she'd packed quite a selection of sarongs. She was almost ready with a cutting remark, but pulled herself up sharply. It wouldn't do to antagonise him. She couldn't take that risk. There was too much at stake.

'Yes, sarongs do spring to mind when you think of the Friendly Islands,' she said, managing to hold on to her self-control, 'but I'll wait and see what the islanders are wearing.'

Twisting her gold wedding band, she recalled her conversation with Adam long before the wedding. She remembered how he'd insisted they marry if he was not to divulge the truth, and how she'd struggled against her feelings of deep apprehension at the mere thought of it.

He'd made it sound so easy, as though both their feelings weren't involved and never would be. But despite the obvious sincerity in his voice, she still wasn't convinced. Surely he could see that there was a downside to what he had proposed. He was leaving out what was, in her opinion, the most important element of all.

'So you don't intend to marry for

love?' she'd enquired.

'I've considered it very carefully,' he said, 'but love's transient, very transient, isn't it? It's a romantic notion, I agree, but I don't think it guarantees a happy marriage, do you?'

He stopped speaking for a moment to test Christine's reaction.

'This marriage will take place because it is necessary. It has little to do with love or romance.'

Christine did her best to think clearly, but was finding great difficulty following his train of thought. Their marriage had little to do with love or romance, he'd said, but how could he be sure that would satisfy him? How could either of them be sure? She'd always imagined that one day she'd find Mr Right, someone she could love and be loved by in return. She'd never contemplated a cold, business arrangement. Even their honeymoon was part of some property deal.

'But surely you'd settle for love,' she argued, 'as long as everything else you required in a marriage fell into place?'

His smiles had done nothing to warm the coldness in his eyes.

'It makes more sense than marrying for love when they're not.'

She couldn't believe he'd settle for a loveless marriage. Surely he'd too much integrity for that. Surely he wouldn't agree to a compromise, and yet it seemed that was what he was prepared to do.

'How can you say that? If you consider the situation long-term, surely you'd want both.'

'That would be ideal, of course, but we don't live in an ideal world. Just think about it, Christine. In these particular circumstances, perhaps it's best if the notion of love is left out of it altogether.'

She bristled with a renewed sense of fear, fear for the future, for what lay ahead. In spite of the fact that he'd talked with conviction, this wasn't what she'd wanted. It wasn't what she'd envisaged for herself at all, and the thought of it knocked her off balance.

'But suppose I don't feel the same?'

'When you've given some serious thought to what's involved you will feel the same, I assure you. We have to accept what this marriage is all about. If we both go into it accepting that certain conditions must be fulfilled, it's much more likely to succeed.'

'You talk as if you want to clinch some cold-hearted business deal.'

'What's wrong with that? If I want a successful future, I want to plan it with as much care as I plan my business deals, in fact with even more care, because I only intend to marry once, which makes it more important.'

He obviously meant what he said. Didn't he intend to go on seeing his mistress then, if he had a mistress! Perhaps that was just hearsay. She didn't know why it should bother her, but amazingly, it did, perhaps because she'd always reckoned on having a husband who would remain faithful to her. But what if she couldn't remain faithful to him? He hadn't considered that as a possibility, had he? She had taken her courage in both hands. After all, she might just as well find out once and for all, and put her mind at rest.

'Even so, things might go wrong,' she said. 'What happens then? Would you agree to an open marriage?' she asked in a tentative voice.

'No, definitely not. I'd stick to my wedding vows and expect my wife to do the same. The fact that it is considered to be a business arrangement would make no difference at all.'

So perhaps she was wrong about him having a mistress. He'd made it perfectly clear he intended to be faithful.

'But a business arrangement seems so unfeeling.'

'Not in this case. Remember, we're only discussing this one particular case. Surely there's no argument about that.'

'Perhaps not, but what if, when it's too late, one of us falls in love with someone else?'

'In the unlikely event of that happening, it would complicate things, of course. But we're both mature and have considered the options, so we wouldn't let it make any difference.'

He paused, indicating that he wanted to end the conversation.

'Knowing what's at stake, especially for you, and realising all the implications, it shouldn't be too difficult for us to stifle unwanted emotions. I'm sure you'll agree with that.'

She felt a sudden, sharp concern. No matter what he'd said or how convincingly he'd said it, she still hadn't been sure that either of them was doing the right thing. How could he commit his whole future to someone whose business ethics he knew his wife despised? It meant, in real terms, that she despised the man himself.

She thought for a moment, trying to make sense of it all. She had to admit he had his good points. To be fair to him, she knew he had qualities she couldn't help but admire. But love? For all his charisma and charm, she couldn't ever imagine loving him, not some hard-headed, shrewd entrepreneur.

Once back at Adam's home, she was quick to fling aside the hated wedding dress. She changed into a sapphire blue trouser suit that matched her eyes. A tap on the door startled her.

'Are you ready, Christine?' her chief bridesmaid said. 'Time's getting on and you've still to throw your wedding bouquet.'

Christine was following her downstairs, when she saw a dark-haired woman in her mid-twenties draping herself over Adam. Her head was thrown back in a gesture of abandon. The champagne glass she was holding was tilted at an angle, the contents spilling on the floor. Seeing Christine, Adam prised the woman's arm from around his neck.

'Christine, this is . . . '

'Debra,' the woman cut in.

'My sister-in-law,' Adam explained.

'Widowed sister-in-law,' Debra contradicted. 'Get it right, Adam. I'm free for any offers. Where's that waiter? I want more champagne.'

'No,' Adam said. 'You've had too much to drink already.'

'Too much to drink? I'll tell you when I've had too much to drink.'

Debra leaned against him, eyeing Christine up and down.

Christine was lost for words. Adam's sister-in-law? She didn't know he had a sister-in-law. Then she remembered hearing him say his younger brother had been killed in a yachting accident. This must be his widow.

'Debra, this is my wife, Christine,' Adam said. 'Perhaps . . . '

Debra blinked as though she was emerging from darkness into bright sunlight.

'Christine,' she repeated. 'Oh, yes, clever Christine. Should I give you your wedding present now? Tell me, when's the happy day?'

'Today, of course,' Adam said before

Christine could answer. 'Today's our wedding day. Don't you realise that's why you're here?'

Once Adam had released her, her balance left much to be desired and she stood swaying gently from side to side.

'Well,' she went on, 'when will you hear the patter of tiny feet?' Then turning to Christine again she continued, 'So, my charming brother-in-law has made an honest woman of you, or maybe you're not an honest woman. Maybe you're no different from all the rest.' She gave a scornful laugh. 'Gold-diggers, the lot of them. Adam's got a reputation for attracting gold-diggers, haven't you, Adam?' She turned to Christine again. 'How come you got to the head of the queue?'

Christine felt a deep blush spread over her face as Adam grabbed his sister-in-law by the arms and tried to shake some sense into her.

'Stop it, Debra. Stop it, do you hear? You're making an exhibition of yourself. Stop it or I'll . . . '

'You'll what? What will you do? Throw me out of the house? You know you can't do that. Your brother wouldn't like it. You wouldn't like it, would you, Stephen, is it?' she shrilled. 'You . . .'

Nigel, Adam's best man, was trying to carry on a normal conversation with a group of wedding guests standing nearby, but was having difficulty making himself heard above the sound of Debra's strident voice.

'Be quiet, Debra,' Adam said. 'You need some fresh-air. Nigel,' he called, 'Debra's not feeling too well. Could you . . .'

'Yes, of course.' Taking in the situation in an instant, Nigel took a firm grip of Debra's hands and guided her out of the room and on to the terrace.

'I don't want fresh air,' she protested to Adam, as she was led away. 'I just want your attention. You won't hold him, you know,' she hissed at Christine. 'He'll go back to his mistress. Did you know he had one? No, I thought not. Well I'll tell you. I . . . '

Adam rushed to Christine's side.

'Christine, are you all right? I don't know how to apologise. Debra's sick. She's drunk as well. She'd no right to speak to you like that. I don't know what came over her. She . . . '

Bemused by Debra's attitude, Christine decided not to pursue the matter further. The woman was obviously besotted with her brother-in-law. Was she always this mean and spiteful, she wondered, or was it because she had married Adam? With her bouquet to throw and a plane to catch, she'd no intention of worrying about her now. Perhaps later . . .

Running to the top of the stairs, she turned her back on the guests assembled in the hall below and threw her wedding bouquet over her head. There were shrieks of laughter as it flew in the air and landed in the arms of one of her bridesmaids.

Adam looked at his watch.

'Come along, Chris, the taxi's arrived.'

The taxi driver took their luggage and, amidst much laughter, Adam and Christine ran towards the waiting car, trying to dodge the shower of confetti.

Fortunately for both of them, Debra was nowhere to be seen.

2

Exhausted by the wedding, the flight and the time difference, Christine was grateful for the overnight stop in Los Angeles, and fell fast asleep the moment her head touched the pillow.

Next morning, she felt revived after her long sleep and she and Adam checked in at Royal Tongan Airlines with plenty of time to spare.

'We're on a scheduled flight to Fua'amotu International Airport on Tongatapu,' Adam said. 'There's time for another coffee if you'd like one.'

'Yes, please. Tell me some more about the island we're making for. Is it completely uncommercialised?'

'Yes, it is, for the present. A lot depends on its potential as a tourist attraction.' Then noting her wry expression he went on, 'Why do you look so disapproving? Have you some special interest in the South Pacific islands that I know nothing about?'

'No, of course not. It's just that I care a great deal about environmental issues, and the thought of a lovely, tropical island being ruined by some crass commercial enterprise is . . . ' She broke off, trying to find the right words.

'I know what you mean,' he said, 'but sometimes you have to learn to compromise. Tell me,' he went on, gazing directly into her dark eyes, 'how did a girl like you become so eco-friendly?'

'It was partly my mother's influence,' she said. 'She founded a movement called Earth First, similar to Friends of the Earth. I helped part-time until she died and then I took over all the organisation. It kept me busy, as I sat on a lot of committees. I've got a degree in environmental studies and have been involved with conservation issues ever since.'

'Earth First.' He thought for a moment. 'An excellent name, I must say. It speaks for itself, doesn't it?' Leaning across the table, he put a tentative hand on her arm. 'I'm sorry about your mother. There's so much about you I still have to find out. But I suppose we've got the rest of our lives for that, haven't we? Now that we're married, I mean. How old were you when she died?'

A cloud passed over Christine's face.

'I was just seventeen. She went on a boating holiday. She'd always been mad about boats. There was an accident and she was swept overboard. My father never really got over it. And I . . . '

'Well, as of now, you can relax, because I assure you things are still in the planning stage. I haven't any definite plans to develop the island,' Adam said, quickly changing the subject. 'Let me tell you a bit about it. The islanders live in two-storey, timber houses with roofed verandas where they sit and watch the world go by. The houses — they're called fales in Tongan, by the way — may be modest by

Western standards, but the island's a tropical paradise, I'm told.

'Oh, yes, and by the way, we've got a housekeeper, a Polynesian woman called Palola. Not a housekeeper in the strictest sense, because she won't be living in our house, but she'll be looking after us. She's lived on the island all her life so she'll be able to answer any questions you may have. I'm told she speaks English, but to what standard I haven't a clue. Apparently she's quite a character. She keeps a strict eye on the natives and knows everything there is to know about the island and its customs.'

Christine was anxious to learn as much as she could about the island. Before she'd fallen asleep on the plane to Los Angeles, she'd started to read a book on Tonga. What she'd read had delighted her, especially the details of the smaller islands, like the one they were heading for. The coral reefs, turquoise water and endless deserted white sandy beaches were a far cry from commercial tourist resorts and towering hotel complexes. Could he be giving serious thought to making such a tranquil island a tourist attraction, she wondered. The mere thought of it appalled her.

Adam went to check the screens for their flight details.

'Our departure gate number has come up,' he said. 'We're on our way.'

They arrived at Tonga's airport without incident, and collected their luggage. The flight was a short one, leaving them with only a short sail to their island.

'The islanders have been expecting you for days,' the ferry-master said. 'You're the honeymoon couple, aren't you? The Kyles?' Then as Adam nodded, 'I thought so. Your reputation's preceded you. The locals are preparing a feast to welcome you to the island.'

Adam stared at him, intrigued.

'A feast? Just for the two of us? That's just great, isn't it, Chris?' he said, turning to Christine for confirmation. 'On such a small island I'm surprised they'd go to so much trouble.'

'The smaller the island, the warmer the welcome,' the ferry-master said. 'It's a matter of pride to the people preparing it.'

'I believe they're letting us stay in one of their houses,' Adam said. 'I hope we're not turning anyone out. We wouldn't want that.'

'Good heavens, no,' the ferry-master replied. 'The locals would be very offended if you stayed somewhere other than their homes. They're generous that way. They'd give you their last cent and never expect compensation, because they're so pleased you've chosen to stay on their island.'

Going to a cupboard, he took out three glasses and a bottle.

'As you're on your honeymoon, it seems a toast is in order. This is some of the local brew. Nothing too sophisti-cated, I'm afraid.'

They thanked him and Adam quaffed it down.

'Wow, it's a killer,' he said, as the

liquid burned his throat. 'What's it called?'

'Kava, made from the root of the pepper plant. It's very potent stuff,' the ferry-master told them. 'I'd be careful if I were you, Mrs Kyle.'

Cautiously Christine took a sip.

'Yes, I see what you mean. It takes your breath away.'

'Will there be someone to help with the luggage?' Adam enquired. 'When you drop us off, I mean.'

'Oh, yes, no worries about that. There will be a look-out at the top of a palm tree who'll tell the others when they see the ferry arrive, and if that doesn't work, coconut wireless will tell them you're on your way.'

Adam looked puzzled.

'Coconut wireless? What on earth's that?'

The ferry-master grinned. 'It's a means of communication in use throughout the islands. Through an amazing system, unknown to Western technology, people all over the islands know what's going on — what foreigners are up to, who is in love with whom, even what the king is doing at the moment and so on. Like I said, it's an amazing system. I've honestly never heard of anything like it.'

'Well, we're learning something every minute,' Christine said, amused.

'Once you get to the island, Palola will look after you,' the ferry-master said. 'Stick with Palola and you won't go far wrong. Now get your things together. We'll be arriving in about ten minutes' time.'

Sure enough, they soon saw a long stretch of endless, deserted white sand, and after wishing them well, the ferry-master dropped them off, and left them standing in a clearing where dozens of coconut palms inclined their fringed heads towards the sparkling beach.

'Have to do something about an airstrip if things go as planned,' Adam said, watching the ferry depart. 'We'll never get tourists to come here without proper luggage-handling facilities. Remind me to make a note of it.'

Good heavens, Christine thought to herself, he's already checking out the island before we've even had time to unpack. He needs to take things slowly, and curb his impatience. Do it the Tongan way — tomorrow! Let's hope he gets the hang of it before we both become nervous wrecks.

Her thoughts were interrupted by the sound of sweet music.

'Am I going crazy?' Adam said. 'I could swear I hear guitars.'

'Me, too,' Christine said. 'And what's that tantalising smell?'

Before either of them could utter another word, a group of islanders approached them, picked up their suitcases and gestured to them to follow. Reaching a clearing, they saw several women carrying big mats woven from coconut frond, piled high with exotic food. They recognised suckling pig, chicken, shellfish, crayfish, yams and sweet potatoes. There were other delights that were entirely Polynesian

35

and they were amazed at the variety on display. Surely this couldn't all be for them?

'I hope not,' Christine whispered to Adam. 'I wouldn't know where to start.'

The men were cooking more food in huge pits in the ground. In the centre of all this activity, a big Polynesian woman with a huge smile and wearing a bright, multi-coloured smock and a battered, wide-brimmed straw hat, was waving her arms, shouting words in Tongan that sounded like instructions — Palola!

Seeing Christine and Adam, she moved towards them with a sashaying walk and outstretched arms, kissed Adam on both cheeks, then moved to Christine and, taking hold of both her hands, held her out at arms' length, all the time grinning from ear to ear.

'Me, Palola,' she said, pointing to herself. 'Talitali fiefia. Welcome.'

Her huge black eyes took in Christine's stylish trouser suit.

'English bride make very fine lady. This my fale,' Palola said, pointing to a conventional Tongan house with a thatched roof which stood amid a forest of coconut palms and pandanus trees.

The charming building was on two levels. It had a porch and a timber veranda, on which a hammock was slung between two palm trees. Christine recognised hibiscus and other tropical plants, which created an oasis of colour among the coconut palms. The air was heady with the erotic, sensuous perfume of frangipani and gardenias.

Glad to relax after the cramped conditions of the ferry boat, she sank down on the hammock, while Adam took out his binoculars and searched the skyline.

'You thirsty?' Palola asked with another beaming smile. 'Here, drink juice of papaya,' and she handed a large glass of the juice to Adam and Christine.

'It's delicious,' Christine said, gulping it down, and holding out her glass for more. 'Tell me, Palola, how did you know we'd arrived? The ferry-master told us you'd been expecting us for days. Yet you sent some islanders to meet us.'

Palola grinned. 'Coconut wireless tell. All island know.' Pointing to the trays of food, she went on, 'Tonight we make feast in your honour. Feast big excuse to meet visitors from England,' Palola went on, showing gleaming white teeth. 'All island come. We sing and dance Polynesian way. We busy cooking food now.'

'Now I take you inside. Bigger house than mine. I show.'

Palola mumbled something in her native tongue to two young islanders, who immediately picked up Christine's and Adam's luggage, and all four of them took up the rear guard and followed Palola across the clearing. Before too long they came to a rickety, wooden bridge.

'See fale over bridge,' Palola said, pointing to the house and sure enough they saw a large thatched building looming up in front of them.

'This doesn't look very safe,' Adam said as they wandered across it carefully.

'Be careful. The slats in this bridge can hardly support it. Good job you're not wearing high heels.'

The men put down their luggage and Palola opened the door, and waited till they went inside.

'I go now. You change clothes and come to feast. I make lei, a garland for you, is custom.'

Without more ado, she and the two men left them to it and walked back over the bridge.

'Well,' Adam said with a grin, 'Palola is some character, isn't she? Let's take a look around the house before we unpack.'

Christine was also anxious to look round and saw that the ground floor was divided into a sitting-room and dining area. The timber floors were not slippery to walk on because they were covered with variously-coloured mats made from coconut frond. Easy-chairs and loungers in a coloured chintz-like material helped to give a relaxed atmosphere, and she found a bar in the dining area stocked with alcoholic drinks as well as the inevitable papaya juice. Upstairs were two large bedrooms and a bathroom with a whirlpool bath and bidet.

'I'm overwhelmed,' Christine exclaimed. 'It's lovely. Don't you think so?'

'Yes. With one or two embellishments it would make an ideal showhouse if the island is developed. Meanwhile, let's unpack and enjoy. We've got to attend this feast they've prepared, and I for one, am going to climb into something less formal.'

Thank goodness he said if about the island rather than when, Christine thought. Perhaps there's still a chance his plans will come to nothing. But now wasn't the proper time to bring such matters to a head and she started to unpack her suitcases. For five minutes or so, she mulled over what would be

40

appropriate to wear, and finally decided on an off-the-shoulder blouse and blue cotton skirt.

Adam was equally informal, in a bright, multi-coloured shirt, which Christine guessed must have been specially bought for such an occasion, and a pair of cream shorts which made him look much younger than his thirty-six years. He was heart-stoppingly handsome, there was no doubt of that, and she could see why women flocked after him. Remembering her unexpected reaction when he had kissed her in church, she thought how easy it would be to succumb to his potent charm.

She pulled herself together quickly when she remembered that he was merely using her. He'd clearly set out his reason for this marriage, and out of loyalty to her father, she'd agreed to go along with it.

They made their way back over the foot-bridge and found Palola waiting for them in the clearing.

'I bring lei like I promise,' she said, placing a garland of multi-coloured flowers round each of their necks. 'Is Polynesian custom. Now, copy me. Feast all ready. I show.'

They watched her sit, crossed-legged, on the ground amid a circle of islanders, and they quickly followed suit. The women, bearing various types of food on the trays made from coconut fronds, stood in front of them waiting to know what they wanted, and Christine had a difficult time deciding.

'Try Tongan speciality,' Palola said. 'You eat with fingers, yes?'

Christine and Adam tucked into a wonderful concoction of corned beef and boiled taro cooked in coconut cream, followed by a delicious breadfruit pudding. Kava and papaya juice were passed round the circle from hand to hand. With the sound of sweet music strumming all around her and after drinking at least three glasses of kava, despite Adam's restraining hand, Christine felt herself relax.

She had never contemplated for a moment a welcome like this and it seemed there was more to come.

'Now you watch,' Palola said. 'Girls dance lakalaka. Is special. Dance only to please guests.'

Clapping her hands, she called out something in her own language, and about two dozen or so young girls formed themselves into two long lines. Hibiscus flowers decorated their hair, while clusters of the same flowers were fastened round their wrists and ankles.

'You watch hands,' Palola said, as the girls started to sway to the strum of guitars. 'Hands tell stories. Take long time to learn. You like?'

Christine watched, fascinated by the sound and movement. The sensual swaying, combined with the hand movements, had a hypnotic effect and were hauntingly beautiful. The music and the dancing were just reaching their climax when a laughing native boy grabbed hold of both Christine's hands. He pulled her to her feet, and soon the pair of them were swaying to the sensual music, the islander holding on to her, refusing to let her go.

This can't be me, she thought, closing her eyes to shut out the lights flashing before them, while the natives clapped and chanted phrases in Tongan she couldn't understand. But it is me, and for the first time in weeks I'm really enjoying myself. Her feet were scarcely touching the ground and her partner stopped dancing and clasped her tightly around the waist. Opening her eyes, she confronted that compelling gaze from the darkest of dark eyes and saw the pursed lips of disapproval.

'Come on, you've had enough,' Adam muttered through clenched teeth as he grasped her arm.

She tried to wrench herself away.

'Stop it. Let go of me. Can't you see I'm enjoying myself?'

But he refused to release her and tightened his grip on her arm. She struggled and planted both feet firmly on the ground, but all to no avail. She couldn't compete with his strength.

'Don't be so stupid,' he grated. 'Try to keep some shred of dignity. We're guests of these people. They're doing their best to entertain us, but you're carrying things too far. Now that you're my wife, is this how you intend to behave?'

Practically dragging her across the wooden bridge, he carried her into the house and sat her down in one of the armchairs. Then he waited for the coffee percolator to work and poured hot coffee down her throat.

'I don't know why you're making such a fuss,' Christine said, trying to swallow the hot liquid. 'They're only a bunch of islanders having a good time.'

She banged her coffee cup down in annoyance.

'There wasn't any need for you to grab me and drag me here against my will. Don't pretend you care about me, because you don't. This wedding, this honeymoon, all of it,' she spat out, 'is just a farce. You blackmailed me into marrying you, and now I'm paying the price.'

Springing out of her chair, she went on, 'You said this marriage wouldn't be like any other. Well, this honeymoon won't be either. It's just a business arrangement, remember? So don't think for one moment you'll be welcome to share my bed!'

3

Christine recalled how she had delayed any decision about marriage until the truth had been proved beyond a reasonable doubt. How to approach Jonathan Childes on such a delicate matter was the next problem she had to confront, and as she sat down to write to him, fear clenched her stomach.

What could she say? Should she send a personal apology for her father's misdemeanour? Only it wasn't just a misdemeanour, was it? It was a crime, punishable by goodness knows how many years in jail.

She had no reason to doubt Adam's honesty, but in this particular instance there was so much at stake. Her whole future, an entire lifetime, was to be given over to this man. The responsibility of agreeing to such a marriage was something she didn't feel she could bear, but when she considered the alternative — her father's name being splashed across the tabloids — there wasn't anything she wouldn't do to prevent it.

She didn't receive a reply from Childes himself. All correspondence relating to his business had been passed to his solicitor to deal with, a firm called Gascoigne & Co. They wrote to her requesting verification of her name and the name of her solicitor, to whom she spoke in the utmost confidence, explaining her position. Once Gascoignes were satisfied, they sent her details of her father's debts to Jonathan Childes, together with the name of the company who settled them, one of Adam's companies, of course, together with the contract of confidentiality that Jonathan Childes had signed.

That done, she knew she would be compelled to marry Adam. She had no choice in the matter. But before she left on her honeymoon she made sure that this confidential information was carefully locked away in the bureau at the house.

When Christine walked in on Adam the morning after the feast, he was helping himself to a myriad assortment of tropical fruits from a large earthenware bowl. Ever since dawn broke, she'd worried about his reaction to her outburst the previous night. Had she gone too far?

She walked slowly into the sitting-room. Facing him after her behaviour the previous night took all the courage she possessed, but she needn't have worried. Dressed in a pair of light blue shorts and a navy and white striped shirt, he looked completely relaxed.

'Hi, how are you feeling this morning?' he enquired. 'Not hung-over, I hope. That kava really gets to you, doesn't it? Would you like some coffee, and a mango perhaps? They're really delicious.'

Realising he wasn't showing any sign of resentment, she began to feel more at ease. Obviously he was mature enough not to hold a grudge. That earned him a few bonus points anyway. She helped herself to a glass of juice and piled it high with ice cubes.

She began in a tentative tone. 'I just want to say . . . ' but he stopped her before she could go on.

'Ssh! Don't say a word. There's no need. It's a brilliant morning and I thought, if you're agreeable, that we might make a tour of the island. My video camera's at the ready and although I've some idea of what the island has to offer, I want to see things for myself.'

'What things?' she enquired, thinking he was back on his development tack.

'Well, the flora and fauna for a start, the undulations in the land, and the possibility of providing an airstrip on the north side, if it's feasible. Tourists would hardly want to put up with those cramped conditions on the ferry, and cabins are at a premium, as you know. In any case, the ferry doesn't cater for dropping tourists off because until now there's never been a call for it.'

He smiled, taking in her pink T-shirt and brief white shorts that showed off her tanned, slender legs to perfection.

'Are you game?'

She managed a brief smile.

'I'm game for anything so long as it doesn't involve drinking kava!'

His eyes crinkled at the corners. 'Anything?'

A deep blush burned her cheeks as invisible sparks flared between them.

'Well, anything that involves the island's conservation issues,' she hastened to add, 'and as you say, it's a glorious day.'

She had heard that the island was never unbearably hot, not even at mid-day, rather it was a pleasant climate, slightly cooler than most tropical areas, only disturbed by the occasional tropical storm.

'Let's go then,' Adam said as he picked up his video camera, his clip-board and pocket memo.

As they walked out into the bright sunlight, Christine could understand why the Polynesian islands were called the land that time forgot. There were no hassles, no hurries, and it seemed that time stood still. As she exposed herself to the lure of the evocative, ginger-scented air, she was overwhelmed by feelings of indolence and torpor she'd never known before.

She discovered later that it happened to everyone who visited the South Seas, and happened quickly, too. Polynesian paralysis, it was called and she'd read about it in one of the brochures. But she hadn't really believed it existed until she had experienced it for herself.

The morning passed easily enough. Adam was absorbed taking photographs, speaking into his pocket memo and scribbling notes, while Christine stared in wonderment at the beauty surrounding her. She was completely shut off in a world of her own when Adam approached her, making her jump.

'I think we'll go back to Palola's house and forage for some lunch,' he said. 'I'm starving.' He laughed. 'Ridiculous, isn't it? After last night, I didn't think I'd want to eat for a week!'

'Me, too,' Christine said, as they walked back to the clearing.

Palola must have anticipated their return because she appeared from nowhere, leading two horses and flanked by two natives carrying a cool-box.

'Plenty left to eat,' she said with a smile. 'In box is baked chicken, suckling pig and papaya juice. Kava too strong for time of day.'

Smiling another of her beaming smiles she went on, 'Cousin lends you horses. You go and explore rest of island. Big shame to waste day, I think.'

'I wonder how she knew we could ride,' Christine remarked, climbing up on a chestnut mare. 'I love horses. I've been around them all my life and at one time we kept stables and I could teach. That's why our house was called Hunters' Lodge.'

Her eyes clouded over at the memory of what she had been forced to leave behind, but she soon regained her composure. She wondered if Adam had noticed the first glimmer of a tear as the horses walked on.

'I know what you mean,' he said, as he hoisted the cool-box in front of him. 'I, too, have a great affection for horses. When I had the time, horses were one of my passions, until work intervened. I must say these two seem very well behaved considering they are being ridden by perfect strangers.'

One of his passions? I wonder what other passions he has, Christine thought. He was a passionate man, no doubt about that, and he'd known many women, she supposed. How long before he was unfaithful, before he tired of this mockery of a marriage? He'd told her that one of his reasons for marrying her was to keep other women at bay, not because he loved her, and yet, if she refused to consummate the marriage, he might not feel it necessary to keep his part of the bargain, maintaining silence about her father. She knew it was in her own best interest to be a proper wife to him.

There were so many things about him she didn't know and had still to find out. They had arranged the wedding so hastily that they still had much to learn about each other.

The weather stayed magnificent, and the beauty of the coral reef they headed for was so overwhelming that her breath caught in her throat. Noticing her preoccupation with her surroundings, Adam shot her an amused glance.

'Dull country,' he quipped. 'Nothing to catch the eye. No hamburger stands, no cyber cafés, no video games. Very uninteresting!'

She laughed.

'No supermarket loyalty cards either!'

After tethering their horses, they sat in the shade of a great banyan tree, the shimmering surf never out of sight, the evocative ginger-scented air tempting them to forget the rigours of civilisation, at least for a while.

'This seems as good a place as any for us to have our lunch,' Christine said, and, shielding her eyes from the sun's glare, she started to smother sunscreen to every inch of skin that was exposed.

'I should think you have to be very careful with a sensitive skin like yours,' Adam said, watching her closely. 'Do you tan easily? Don't forget the parts you can't see. Here, allow me.'

He took the bottle from her hand, and started to apply the sunscreen to the back of her neck. The thrill of his touch as he smoothed the liquid into her neck and shoulders tingled throughout her whole body and down her spine. There was something about the way he was touching her that turned her body. She knew it was having the same effect on him, for his hand trembled.

He stopped abruptly and handed the bottle back to her.

'It's time you returned the compliment,' he said.

She felt her skin burn with hot colour.

'If you insist,' she said, but aware of her response to him, her hands barely skimmed over his skin before she made the excuse of opening the cool-box.

'Hey, this tastes good.'

Adam finished a spicy chicken leg and poured papaya juice for them both.

'Palola certainly knows how to look after us.'

Christine smiled her agreement.

'It's like the ferry-master said. Visitors are always well looked after in the South Seas. It's tradition.'

They ate the food with a good appetite, licking their fingers clean and quaffing the juice Palola had placed in the cool-box. Then they lay on their backs and gazed up at the fringed heads of the sheltering palms. Christine didn't want to move, she felt so carefree and relaxed. When she did eventually, and rested on her elbows, she found herself gazing into a pair of dark brown eyes.

She wondered what he was thinking

about. Was it this calm, relaxed atmosphere so typical of the Friendly Islands with their lavish hospitality and Polynesian charm, or was it the potential for commercial development that filled his thoughts? He was so difficult to understand. His nature was so complex most of the time, but at other times, she could have sworn he understood her point of view about the island even if he would never accept it.

She mused on for a while, enjoying the balmy breeze that swept through the gigantic banyan trees. If only things had been different, she could have accepted him as a husband, but while she despised him and his ambition, acceptance was out of the question.

Shifting her gaze, she studied him out of the corner of her eye. He looked magnificent, there was no doubt about it, and her heart gave a leap when she imagined what it would be like to lie in his arms on this sandy beach, with the waves crashing on to the shore and the pungent scent of the hibiscus all around them. She lifted her face towards the sun in an attempt to push such thoughts out of her mind, but she felt compelled to gaze at Adam again, almost against her will. He was smiling, his eyes half-closed. He murmured something as he fingered the pink frangipani blossom she wore in her hair.

'You're wrong, you know,' he said. 'You've made a mistake with that flower, putting it behind your left ear. In the Friendly Islands it isn't the thing to do.'

Christine looked up, surprised.

'What do you mean, it isn't the thing to do? I think the frangipani is beautiful. Don't you approve?'

Adam grinned. 'I approve of the flower, all right. It's lovely, but I don't approve of where you've put it. I don't suppose you gave it much thought.'

He plucked the flower gently from behind her left ear.

'You see, you're not the only one who's read the guide books. I've read them, too, and in one of them, it says that when a girl places a flower behind her left ear it means, well . . . '

He broke off, twisting the stem.

'Yes? Go on, I'm intrigued.'

'It means she's unattached. She's still looking.'

'How clever of you to have worked that one out,' Christine said. 'And behind her right ear?'

'It means hands off, she's taken. She's met the man of her dreams, and if your flower wilts quickly, it means you're a flirt.'

Adam leaned forward, and placed the blossom behind her right ear.

The man of her dreams, Christine thought. If only that were true! Adam was the man of many other women's dreams, there was no doubt of that. It had been proved time and time again, and they'd marry him like a shot just to prove they'd got his scalp! But as for her . . .

She watched him stretched out on the sand. How could she reconcile the shrewd, hardheaded business tycoon with the gentle, relaxed male who had momentarily switched off from his entrepreneurial deals to revel in the beauty and timelessness of the island? The side of himself he was displaying now was closer to her heart, but how long could he keep it up? Didn't he realise that the island should remain as the islanders wanted it, without the clamour and crudeness of a commercial enterprise? It was a tribute to nature amid the glory of the South Seas. If only he realised that, maybe there was some hope for this marriage after all.

Having placed the blossom where he wanted it, Adam pulled her towards him gently with an easy strength, his arms tightening around her, his lips seeking her soft mouth.

'Here's to this moment,' he murmured against her skin, 'and to the moments yet to come.'

She felt spellbound, and a trembling of greeting rippled through her as she drew in a shaken breath. The next moment, he drew away.

'Seems we've got company,' he said, gently releasing her as a solitary islander appeared through the trees carrying his primitive fishing tackle.

Giving them a cheery wave, he continued his journey up to the top of the reef. They watched as he baited his line and cast it into the ocean.

'He'll have to move away from there sooner or later,' Adam said sharply, as the man waited patiently, grasping his line. 'According to my draft plan, we intend to develop that site with our new homes. Should be very profitable, bearing in mind the view.'

The spell broken, Christine sprang to her feet. She felt as though Adam had slapped her in the face. How could he think that way? Didn't he realise what a mistake it would be to commercialise the island?

How quickly he'd reverted to the Adam Kyle she'd read about when anything concerned with profit was at stake. He didn't really care about the future of the islanders. He'd proved that by what he'd just said.

'That's where you're wrong,' she seethed. 'The islanders only want to live in peace. There must be few places in the world so completely unspoiled.'

She spoke passionately, with conviction and straight from the heart. But not for one moment did that stop him from punching home his points.

'I don't want to get into an argument about it, Chris,' he said. 'You already know one of my reasons for being here, and in any case, the islanders are very hospitable. How do you know they'll object to a carefully-thought out development scheme? Have you asked them? No. I've given it a great deal of thought and I'm convinced the island can be developed without upsetting anyone or losing its natural charm.'

He stood up, moving slightly away from her, and gazed intently into her eyes.

'What more can I say to convince you?'

'If I were you I wouldn't try,' she answered scornfully.

'Well, I intend to try. From the start of our relationship, you've got these preconceived ideas about me, and from what you've just said it seems you never intend to let them go.'

Making an attempt to control his voice, he said in a softer tone, 'I intend to take all the factors into consideration, see the results from my video camera and have comprehensive plans drawn up. Only after all those things have been accomplished will I make up my mind about any potential development.'

If looks could have killed, he would have dropped dead on the spot.

'I don't know why you chose to bring me here if that's your intention,' she said. 'And if you think I'll be a party to it, you're wasting your time.'

'Being in a place like this is never a waste of time,' he replied, starting to pack the cool-box and placing it on his horse's saddle.

Then he stopped what he was doing and stared out at the thunderous ocean, the great banana plantations and the forest of coconut palms, and went on, 'I've never been closer to paradise.'

Planting both feet firmly on the ground, Christine glared at him.

'A paradise you want to spoil and ruin. Despite what you say, my gut reaction is that I haven't been wrong about you. You're entirely ruthless, aren't you?'

'When it's something involving business, yes, entirely ruthless.'

The cynicism of his words reflected the resentment in her eyes, and she felt she couldn't listen to much more.

'Why are you so pig-headed, Chris?' he went on. 'Surely we can discuss this like two intelligent human beings. I . . . '

'No!'

She shook her head emphatically, and, untethering her horse, she mounted and rode away along the bleached white sand, hair flying, eyes filled with tears, disillusion seeping through every pore.

'Hey, wait for me,' Adam called after her.

But his words were lost on the wind and the sound of the breakers crashing against the coral reef.

4

Darkness fell as a cloak of humid air as Christine stood on the veranda trying to calm her turbulent senses. The flowers of the hibiscus contrasted strongly with the tropical leaves and vines, and she inhaled the sweet smell of the gardenia whose flowers gleamed like stars amid the glossy dark leaves.

After she'd left her horse tethered safely outside Palola's house, she'd clambered across the wooden foot-bridge, and found refuge in one of the two bedrooms. She felt better when she'd changed into a cotton robe, and now she marvelled at the sight she beheld from her own front door. The scents, diverse but never cloying, heightened her senses, and the sound of the surf breaking on to the beach lulled her into a tropical euphoria.

She recalled the pang of pleasure

she'd felt when Adam had kissed her. With hindsight, she couldn't contemplate what might have happened if the fisherman hadn't disturbed them. A good job he did, she thought. Goodness knows where it might have led, but Adam couldn't hide the fact that he wanted her, and in that brief moment she'd realised that, if she'd given way to it, it could have been a passion shared. Her body still thrilled at the memory.

When she'd tried to explain the adverse affect his proposals would have on the island, however, she hadn't been able to reach the cold recesses of his heart. It was as though she were trying to reach him through a sheet of glass.

When he'd seen the fisherman high up on the reef, she'd expected a completely different reaction. She thought he'd appreciate the fact that fishing, Polynesian style, was one of the fascinating features of the place, but instead of accepting that such primitive pleasures possessed a certain charm, he'd merely pointed out that the man could be forced to leave.

She had no intention of losing her self-control the way she had. She'd merely tried to state her case, but in retrospect her outburst made her feel stupid and immature. Why had she involved herself in that kind of childish sparring?

Deep in reverie, she jumped when she heard a soft tread behind her, and she didn't need to turn round to know that it was Adam. Placing a tentative arm around her shoulders, he turned her gently to face him.

'You've got very strong views about the island, haven't you?' he said.

'Yes, I have. I can't remember a time when I wasn't committed to preserving the countryside, wild life and natural things. Perhaps I inherited it from my mother.'

He gazed at her intently. 'Point taken.'

'I'm sorry I lost my temper. I shouldn't have done. I . . . '

'And I made an unfortunate remark,'

he interrupted, 'and I'm sorry about that, too.'

Sitting her down on the hammock that swung between two palm trees, he sat down next to her.

'But really, you've got me all wrong. If the island is developed at some future time, and I say if, every effort will be made to fit in with the existing environment, and not the other way round. In any case, the Tongan Planning Authority would have to approve any plans, so there won't be any big tower blocks, burger-bars or all-night discos. Just the reverse, in fact. If and when the plans are drawn up, I'll let you see them. Trust me.'

His dark eyes gazed into hers with such intensity that she wanted to believe him with all her heart.

'Trust is a mutual thing,' she said. 'After the way I've behaved, you may have as little faith in me as you believe I have in you.'

For answer he put a finger to his lips. 'No more talk of that,' he said. 'Let's discuss what we'll do tomorrow. I thought it might be a good idea to take a look at Nuku'alofa, unless you've something else in mind. We could . . . '

Relieved he was in such a good humour, Christine would have agreed to almost anything.

'Yes, that would be lovely,' she said. 'There's so much to see. But how would we get to the mainland?'

'No problem. Coconut wireless,' Adam said cheerily. 'I thought I'd take advantage of it. Apparently the islanders have some way of contacting the cruise ships and ferry boats. As luck would have it, one's heading in our direction and should arrive just after dawn. It won't be any trouble at all for it to call at the island and pick us up.'

Christine looked puzzled.

'Why did you bother with coconut wireless? You could have used your lap-top and sent the ferry master an e-mail. In any case, it's only the islanders who know about those things.

How did you understand what coconut wireless said?'

'I didn't. Palola did. When I returned the horse, she said it would be a good idea for us to visit Nuku'alofa, and strangely enough she echoed my thoughts exactly. It's weird, isn't it? She's got some kind of mental radar. She knows what you're thinking before you do.'

'I suppose you could put it down to intuition,' Christine replied, 'but who can tell? The island's a paradise, pure and perfect, with an environment as unique as its beauty. Still, it'll be interesting to stroll round Nuku'alofa. Although I've read about it I don't really know what to expect. Is there anything particular on your list of must sees?'

Adam smiled. 'As a matter of fact, there is. You're not a vegetarian, I hope, because there's a very fine sea-food restaurant I thought we might try. I've been reading about it in one of the guides the ferry-master gave me.'

'Is it upmarket, this restaurant of yours?' Christine enquired. 'I don't think a T-shirt and jeans . . . '

'Well, I'm certainly not taking my wife to somewhere cheap and cheerful,' he said, repressing a smile. 'I'll leave it up to you to decide what to wear. Meanwhile, as we'll be doing plenty of walking tomorrow, I suggest we get an early night.'

He kissed her gently on both cheeks, and a dangerous flare of need took over her body. As he walked towards his bedroom door, she felt remorse stab at the very centre of her being. Would he make some move towards her now that she was in a more relaxed state of mind? Would he demand his marital rights knowing she had no right to refuse him? Surely he must have been aware of her response, but maybe he thought it was just as case of conscience, for he made no attempt to capitalise on the situation.

'Do you want to . . . ' she asked in a hesitant voice. 'I mean, should we . . . '

He shrugged. 'You're my wife. I want to take you to bed and make love to you, but now is not the proper time. Get some sleep, Chris. I'll see you in the morning,' and before she could utter another word, he closed his bedroom door.

As Chris lay down alone in the darkness, she tried to ignore the agitated beating of her heart. Saying he wanted to make love to her was not the same as saying he loved her, not by any means. And if she were honest, she knew she longed for love. It wasn't as if she was cold and unfeeling. She had a passionate nature and knew she could express it in the right circumstances and with the right man. But so far, passion had been disappointing and short-lived, and she had not reached the heights she knew in her heart she was capable of reaching.

She'd never met anyone like Adam. How could she have done? She'd never mingled with her father's clients and she had been surprised when he'd brought Adam home to dinner that evening. Her mouth had trembled a little when she saw him, but her eyes had been wary.

'Christine will show you round,' her father had said, 'while I pour the drinks. Brandy, I believe you said.'

He can't appreciate Hunters' Lodge, Christine had thought to herself. His life revolved around the city. He wouldn't appreciate country ways. Was he just paying lip service to it when he admired the library and the sitting-room with their superb views? She had been determined not to show him upstairs. The bedrooms were out of bounds as far as he was concerned, but she noticed that he gave a nod in the direction of the fine, curving staircase, and she led him back to her father's study with a sigh of relief.

Had he been sizing the house up then, she wondered now. Had he more than an inkling of her father's financial situation? Was that why he was so anxious to be given the guided tour?

She had to admit that his attractiveness disturbed her, and perhaps, if the circumstances had been different she might have fallen under his spell like all those women she'd read about.

Her mind returned to the present. Now that she had taken her marriage vows she hoped that, when the time came to consummate the marriage, he would not find her wanting.

You must stop these foolish thoughts, she told herself. You married him because there was no other way out of an untenable situation. It's time to face the truth, and the truth was that he would never love her, but was merely using her. This marriage was one of convenience only, fuelled by his desire to keep predatory females at bay.

She rose at dawn, showered and dressed, and as she walked into the lounge, Adam was waiting for her, looking strikingly lean and handsome. As he handed her a glass of chilled papaya juice, the expression in his eyes made it perfectly clear he approved of what he saw.

She was dressed in a sea-green cotton sundress, and her hair, freed from the pony tail, hung in a cascade down her back. The scent of the perfumed shower-gel she had used still clung to her skin.

'You smell gorgeous,' he said, as the perfume reached his nostrils. 'Here, help yourself to some of these mangoes. They're delicious, and drink that papaya juice. I don't know about you, but I can't face anything else so early in the day.'

She drank the juice.

'How are we for time?' she asked. 'Are you quite happy about the ferry? I'm still not convinced that coconut wireless works. I don't know what to make of it.'

'Have faith,' he said. 'If the ferry doesn't turn up and we can't do it today, we'll do it the Tongan way — tomorrow! There's really nothing to worry about. We're an ocean away from deadlines, hassles and headaches. 'I think we've got everything we need for the day, so we'd best be on our way.'

Walking by Adam's side along the beach, Christine could see the ferry-boat had dropped anchor and was waiting for them to board. They recognised the ferry-master as the same man who had dropped them off when they first arrived at the island, and when he saw them he waved, welcomed them on board, and asked them how they were going to spend their day.

'We've got our own ideas,' Adam said, 'but I'm sure you'll be able to give us some good advice. What's Nuku'alofa like?'

The ferry-master thought for a moment.

'I suppose you could call it Tonga's big smoke,' he said. 'It's still a leisurely place by your standards, but it's got all the trappings of a small-scale big city, if that's not a contradiction of terms. It's got shops, restaurants, travel agents, hotels — the lot!'

Adam looked impressed. 'And where do you suggest we start?'

'The waterfront's as good a place as any, as you can see the royal palace from there. It's a big, white Victorian, timber building surrounded by lawns and pines. You can't miss it. Unfortunately, visitors are not allowed inside, but you can get a good view from the waterfront. The king celebrates his birthday on the fourth of July and the capital will be humming. Also, the Visitors' Bureau on Vuna Road is well worth a visit, and the Prime Minister's residence is quite close. And don't forget the flea market. It sells just about everything.'

As they approached the waterfront, Adam and Christine waved him good-bye after thanking him for his advice.

'Don't like the look of that sky,' he called down to them as they prepared to go ashore. 'Hope there isn't a storm brewing.'

'There's the royal palace,' Christine called out excitedly. 'That big white building. Can you see it? What a pity we can't look inside.'

'It's probably a good thing, or we'd never see anything else,' Adam said with a laugh, 'especially as we're catching the last ferry home. We're lucky it leaves Nuku'alofa so late. Gives us time to look around and finish with a leisurely meal.'

'At that special restaurant you picked out,' Christine said.

'Exactly. Now let's get a move on, there's lots to see. Let's start with the Visitors' Bureau. They'll probably give us some idea of what we should see in such a short time.'

'What road did he say it was on? Let's get a street map so we can find our way around.'

They found the Visitors' Bureau very easily and when the man in charge was told they were only in the capital for the day, he said he would help them as much as he could.

'I'm glad you're so interested,' the Tongan said. 'Please leave your name and address on the visitors' roll. We like to keep a record of visitors, their names and where they come from.'

'Well,' Adam said amused, 'we come from a very small island. You won't have heard of it. In fact we're the only two visitors there, but the islanders treat us like royalty mainly due to the fact that we're on our honeymoon.'

The Tongan beamed with delight.

'In that case, you'll both appreciate the seclusion,' he said. 'My view is that the smaller islands should remain as they are, completely unspoiled. Well, that's just my opinion, for what it's worth. Now are you sure I can't help you further? I see you've got some guide books.'

'No, you've been very kind,' Adam said. 'We can find our way all right. Thanks for your help.'

'Well, that's one in the eye for you,' Christine said, as they walked in the afternoon sunshine. 'Perhaps that Tongan and I should form an alliance. What do you think?'

'I think you should shut up about it,' Adam replied, with a grin. 'Time's short, so let's see as much of the capital as we can.'

Both were suffering from hunger pangs by the time evening came round.

'The fish restaurant I told you about is close to the harbour,' Adam said, 'and one of their specialities is spring lobster. I think I'd be tempted to wash it down with a fine, chilled muscadet. No more kava, I promise you!'

The night sky had changed to a vivid purple and the Pacific glittered like a jewel as they sat on the veranda in flickering candlelight admiring the table which was beautifully decorated with hibiscus and gardenias.

'Good gracious! What a selection,' Adam said, ploughing through the menu. 'I hardly know what to choose.'

When she'd made her choice, she had time to look around her. The wooden bar looked as if it had been constructed from the bow of a boat, and was cluttered with wine bottles of all shapes and sizes. Half a dozen fishing nets were strung across the ceiling, amid an array of lobster pots. Great fish tanks containing various species lined the whole length of one wall, and there was fishermen's diving gear, replicas of huge sea turtles standing on plinths and endless sea shells and sea anemones.

'Look at that.'

Christine had spied a figure of King Neptune, with trident in hand and lashing tail, looking down on the diners from high above the bar.

'He's huge! This really is a unique restaurant.'

'I agree. It's an experience eating here, isn't it?' Adam said, tucking into one of the specialities of the house. 'You can imagine how much planning and thought has gone into this setting, can't you?'

The food was delicious, and the atmosphere friendly and full of good humour, but as Christine's feelings of happiness soared, she had to admit that it had little to do with the atmosphere. Rather it was on account of the man who had brought her here. Finishing his cognac, Adam looked out into the night and held his hand out, palm uppermost.

'I could swear I felt rain,' he remarked. 'Better get inside before it wets us through.'

He was right. In no time at all, a storm was breaking all around them, bending the crowns of the coconut palms on the quay.

'I've heard about these tropical storms,' Adam said. 'Short-lived, but terrifying while they last. I'd better make sure the ferry intends to put out tonight.'

'Take care,' Christine said, as he walked away.

She tried to take her mind off the storm by surveying the great fish tank, the lobster pots and fishing nets, but she couldn't relax when she didn't know if Adam, out in the thick of the storm, was safe or not.

What if he couldn't find the ferryboat, she thought. What if they were stranded? Half an hour passed, then an hour, and still he hadn't returned. What if he'd had an accident, been injured, was lying somewhere where nobody could reach him?

She despised his business commitments, but when she thought of him out in the raging elements, she was being besieged by a welter of very different emotions. She'd just reached breaking point when the door burst open, and, tousled, rumpled and drenched to the skin, Adam stumbled into the restaurant.

His shirt was soaked through and clung to him like a second skin. His hair, wind-strewn and dishevelled, gave him a wild, tempestuous look that was both reckless and exciting.

'Adam! Are you all right?' I've been out of my mind with worry.'

The words trembled on Christine's lips as he took a few paces towards her and held out his arms. Uttering a little cry, she ran into them, fear, relief and panic making her breathless. He cupped her face in his hands, and she could feel his heart pounding through his palms.

'I'm all right but I'm wetting you through,' he said, putting her away from him. 'It's mad out there. No chance of a ferry tonight. No boats are putting out, not even the cruise ships. Fortunately, there's a hotel adjacent to this restaurant. I've had a word with the manager and he's fixed us up with a room for the night. It's en-suite, too, so I'll be able to take a shower.' He grasped her hands. 'Come on, I can't wait to get out of these wet clothes.'

Christine followed him along a corridor which led to the other part of the building which was the hotel. They walked up two flights of stairs and along another corridor, Adam trying to find a room with the number that matched the one on his key. At last they found it. Although quite lavishly appointed with loungers and a small bar and ice cabinet, the bedroom boasted only one bed!

'Where's the bathroom?' Adam said.

Flinging his wet clothes on to the floor, he found it and turned on the shower, not before Christine had a close-up of his naked back, broad shoulders and neat derrière! She felt hot colour rising in her cheeks. From outside the shower cabinet she could see steam rising and the outline of Adam's toned, masculine body as he lathered himself.

'Christine!'

Sliding open the door of the shower cabinet, he called her and made wild gesticulations in her direction. Hardly daring to breathe, she rushed towards him. Whatever was the matter?

'Towel, please.'

Picking up a large, white bath sheet she held it out to him, and he grabbed the end of it and pulled it hard, so that she fell into the shower cabinet to join him. Her befuddled brain raced into shock, as the water jets drenched her.

'What do you think you're doing?' she gasped. 'Don't . . . '

But he took no notice and pulled her towards him. It all happened so quickly that she was hardly aware of him reaching behind her to feel for the zip of her dress, or feel the sodden garment sliding down until it lay at her feet.

'It's more fun with two,' he quipped as the water poured over them.

Then, holding her tightly, he stumbled out of the shower and almost flung her on to the bed.

'I don't want . . . ' she began, as he quickly dried them both with one of the fluffy towels, but she had no option but to give in.

She was suddenly vulnerable, heart-stoppingly female, as a million sensations exploded in her head. She was his wife. At last she acknowledged it, and rejoiced in being under his control.

'Have you ever felt like this before?' he murmured against her skin, and as he clasped her to him, she felt safe and secure in his arms.

5

'I must be dreaming,' Christine murmured, as the morning sun streamed in through the window, and she stirred, stretching her arms above her head.

Opening her eyes, she found herself alone. She slid her arm along the bed. The place next to her was empty. Adam must have gone outside to investigate.

As they walked down to the quay after a light breakfast, there was little sign of the havoc Christine expected to see after the tropical storm. But as it was nearing mid-day, most of the debris down by the quay had been cleared away.

'There's a ferry leaving in about half an hour, according to my reckoning,' Adam said, 'and I suggest we get there in plenty of time. As soon as we get the nod from the ferry-master, we can get on board.'

'That storm last night, a dreadful business,' the ferry-master said when they found him. 'I said I didn't like the look of the sky. Still, I'm relieved to see both of you are still in one piece. Storms like that happen rarely in this part of the world, so I hope you won't be deterred from visiting our capital again. The king's birthday would be a good time. You could see the festival.'

'Yes, we'll look forward to that,' Adam replied, 'although the storm did take us by surprise. But, yes, we're most impressed by what we've seen and we'll certainly come back.'

'Well, I hope you enjoyed your short visit. I'm afraid you saw the capital under the worst conditions, and it was a shame you couldn't get back. I assume you managed to get some accommodation. Many tourists were stranded, I'm afraid.'

'Yes, I know,' Adam said. 'We were two of the lucky ones, and we're anxious to know how our island's been affected. Have you heard how it weathered the storm?'

'As a matter of fact I have,' the ferry-master said. 'I thought you'd ask. Nobody was hurt, by all accounts, but there was quite a lot of damage to the roofs of the houses, although your housekeeper's house is still intact. I've taken a load of supplies on board, so that the roofs can be repaired as quickly as possible in case there's any more rain, though that's most unlikely. It's the far-flung islands that came off the worst, three small volcanic islands in the extreme northern reaches of Tonga. The population's only about three thousand, and the solitude of their environment has given the people a distinctly mellow attitude towards their visitors. Anyone visiting will never feel their efforts have gone unrewarded.'

When they reached the island, they waited while the roofing supplies were unloaded then made straight for Palola's house. Seeing them approach, she sashayed towards them, giving them one of her beaming smiles.

'You're both safe,' she said. 'Storm a terrible thing. There's my cousins,' she went on, indicating half a dozen or so islanders standing in a group. 'Roofs gone. They stay with me. You stay, too. Bridge gone in storm. You no get to fale. You come and see.'

Palola walked ahead and Adam and Christine saw that the wooden bridge had collapsed and had been swept away. A number of islanders were trying to effect repairs, but even if they'd had enough timber, it was obvious it couldn't be completed in one day.

'Why aren't they repairing their own roofs with such materials as they've got,' Christine asked, 'instead of bothering about the bridge?'

'Visitor's fale more important, so bridge must be repaired first,' Palola explained. 'You stay with me. I give you mats to sleep on, same as cousins. Very comfortable. Not so comfortable as big bed though.' She laughed.

The materials were still lying on the sand where they had been dumped, and another group of islanders were standing around surveying it, obviously wondering what to do next.

'I think we need to get some organisation into this,' Adam said, when he saw the Tongans staring at the timber and thatch, 'or it will take for ever to get things done. Better see if I can lend a hand.'

Using Palola as his interpreter, he organised the men into several groups and found out how many of the houses needed repairs. He drew circles in the sand in the centre of which Palola sketched the name of each islander in large letters.

'Now we know how many houses are involved and who owns then,' Adam said in a satisfied tone. 'It's a start.'

He stood back for a moment as the islanders clapped and shouted and shook his hand. He then divided the timber and thatch into separate piles, depending on how many houses were involved.

'I see what you do, but your fale

first,' Palola said, after the timber needed for the bridge had been put on one side.

Adam organised a simple work schedule, and traced the details in the sand, while Palola chatted away to the men in their own language, making sure they took the correct amount of timber to repair the bridge and Adam's and Christine's house.

When all the materials had been carted to the bridge, and the repairs were almost complete, Adam pulled off his shirt, managed to cross the bridge, and started to work on the roof of his house.

'You careful now,' Palola called to him when she saw him climbing up. 'You not used to climb. Let cousins climb.'

But Adam insisted. With his bare chest and with sweat pouring down his face, Christine was seeing a different side of him. Where was the suave businessman now? He was labouring with the same enthusiasm as the islanders. Watching him toiling away doing everything he could to assist, while shouting encouragement to the others, Christine realised just how much she'd underestimated this man, and her heart soared. If only he could see the islanders through her eyes, she thought. Having been instrumental in effecting the repairs, surely he wouldn't contemplate commercial development now. But he was a stubborn, persistent, tenacious man, who would be certain to go ahead with his scheme for the island if there was a profit in it, and there was nothing she could do to stop him.

While the men were working, the women had prepared a meal, and soon the smell of suckling pig and baked chicken proved too much of a temptation. They stopped for a breather, sitting in their usual circle on the ground.

'They've worked hard today,' Adam said, watching them tuck in. 'As for me, I'm using Palola's shower. Then I'm going to dig in to some of that delicious corned beef cooked with coconut. It's a speciality of theirs, Palola said. Care to join me?'

'Do your muscles ache? You're stooping a bit,' Christine said later, as he staggered out of the shower.

'I don't feel too bad now, but I'm going to ache tomorrow,' he said. 'I've used muscles I haven't used for years.'

When they rejoined the others, Christine sat in the circle of islanders and Adam wasn't far behind. Their appetites sated, Adam and Christine wandered off along the beach, the sky now a vivid purple. Taking his hands in hers, Christine ran a finger along the palms.

'Your hands will be covered in callouses if you're not careful,' she told him. 'These are not workman's hands.'

Freeing his hands, he traced the line of her cheekbone and tilted her chin.

'I appreciate your concern,' he said, 'and I wish it was genuine, but I know what you think of me. What you really think.'

'Really think? What do you mean?'

'You think I'm some black-hearted villain who coerced you into marriage, put people out of work and use them for my own ends. Isn't that true?'

'Well,' she began, but he quickly interrupted.

'And the same goes for all my so-called lovers,' he went on. 'Naturally, as a single man, I've had to be seen about town with some famous women. It's good publicity, you see, and my companies need to be kept in the public eye.'

He stopped speaking and took her hand.

'But I want you to know that most of what you've read about me is just paper talk.'

'And those women you've supposedly been involved with?'

'Is nonsense, absolute nonsense. But the point is, it sells newspapers, doesn't it?'

Kissing the centre of her soft palm, he continued, 'To be truthful, I've only ever once been involved in what you would call a serious relationship. But now that's all changed. I'm sure you will agree that no relationship is more serious than marriage.'

Despite what he'd just told her, Christine was still confused. He was probably speaking the truth. He had just been involved in a publicity machine, but what was the one serious relationship he'd referred to? She was determined to find out.

'I suppose you're referring to Debra,' she said. 'Your one serious relationship, I mean. Were you very hurt when she married your brother?'

'Good heavens, no! I'm very fond of Debra, but that's where it ends, and I look after her now because she's family and she's alone.'

Picking up a tendril of Christine's hair, he twisted it round his finger.

'Debra's a lovely girl but she isn't my type. There's never been anything between us although . . . '

'Although she tried to make it look as

if there is,' Christine finished for him. 'She made it obvious she's jealous of me. Oh, I know she'd had a lot to drink, but a woman has an instinct about these things. She'll never accept me as your wife. She'll make trouble.'

'Hush. Let's not talk about her. She's no threat to you, I promise.'

Anxious to believe him, Christine lay down on the sand, the cool southerly breeze gliding across her face like some tropical fan, removing to some extent at least, the gnawing doubts that had haunted her. Adam sprawled out beside her slowly and very gently, with a depth of feeling she hardly recognised.

Helping her to her feet later, they walked in silence towards Palola's house, and to the privacy of their room, where they lay side by side on the soft mattresses, their fingers inter-twined and on the threshold of sleep, Christine felt herself relax as the foam-crested waves pounded against the coral reef.

6

The following few days were spent in limbo. Adam and Christine couldn't return to their own house until the bridge had been repaired and reinforced so that it would not be swept away, however harsh the storm.

As Christine was unable to go to her bedroom to fetch one of the many lengths of cloth needed to make a sarong, she asked Palola if one of the native girls could lend her one. Almost immediately, a length of multi-coloured cloth in varying shades of red and gold was produced. Christine tried to wrap it around her body amid much laughter from a nearby group of female islanders, anxious to see what she would make of it.

'Do I do it this way or that?' Christine exclaimed as the material kept falling to the ground.

The girls giggled, whispering to each other in their own language, then one girl, less cautious than the rest, picked it up and started to wind it around Christine's body. Christine smiled and gathered up the free end. She wriggled out the other end and tied the ends together in a knot between her breasts, so that the sarong looked like a strapless sundress.

The girls laughed and applauded, and Christine walked over to where Adam was lying in a hammock slung between two palm trees. He, too, clapped his hands when he saw her.

'Very amusing,' he said, 'you look like a typical islander with your straight, tanned back and smooth, swaying walk.' He gave her a brief smile. 'So many things have happened in such quick succession,' he went on, 'that we haven't really had time to court each other.'

What a strange thing to say, Christine thought. Get to know each other was more colloquial. The term he had used was more reminiscent of her parents' era!

She sighed when she thought of their lives — her mother, whose life had been drastically cut short, and her poor father who had been driven to commit fraud. She knew she had Adam to thank for pulling him out of the mire, or rather, one of his companies had, which amounted to the same thing.

He'd told her his reasons for marrying her and she knew she could depend on him keeping quiet about her father's transgressions, and now that she'd kept her part of the bargain, she felt she could relax. The marriage had been consummated in a way she wouldn't have thought possible when they'd met on that fateful day at Hunters' Lodge and he'd told her of his future plans.

'Our house is practically ready for occupation,' he said, shifting his position on the hammock and rubbing the bottom of his spine. 'Ouch,' he said, 'I'm still stiff. These islanders are more agile than I am, younger, too. They don't seem to have suffered any repercussions from all that heaving and climbing.'

He got out of the hammock and stretched.

'I was hoping we'd be able to return to our house today,' he said, 'but Palola won't hear of it. She insists on cleaning the place from top to bottom before we go back, so it's frond mattresses again tonight, I'm afraid. I suppose I could walk over and pick up my laptop. There's bound to be some e-mails, but, on second thoughts, I think I'll do it the Polynesian way — when I feel like it!'

Christine glanced up, amused. That was something she'd never expected him to say. It was as though the savage lion had become a purring hearthside cat. Was this committed workaholic revelling in procrastination? If so, there was hope for him yet. But there were still questions to be asked. Couldn't her father's business, now under new management, prosper just as much if she'd been an executive director instead of a wife?

'No,' he'd protested firmly when she tried to have it out with him. 'No, you must accept my terms if your father's culpability is not to become public knowledge. I have my reasons for marrying you, and now we are man and wife I give you my word that no-one will ever discover the truth. Remember, legal contracts are involved, a business contract between Jonathan Childes and myself and a marriage contract between you and me. Those facts are indisputable.'

Christine had always wanted to find out something more of her new husband's background, and now seemed the ideal time to do it.

'Was your father a successful businessman?' she ventured, propping herself against a palm tree. 'Was it because of his influence that you're so ambitious? I realise that you understand the legalities of things. Did you train to be a lawyer?'

'Good guess, but I didn't remain one for long. After my mother left my father for another man, I was told I had to learn about the business, so I had to put aside my aspirations and knuckle down to it. I wasn't given any choice.'

'I see now why you insisted on marrying me,' she said. 'You wanted someone who would not only enter into a legal commitment, but who would never dare to cheat on you, someone who had something to fear. A strange motivation for a successful marriage, I should think.'

'Stop it, Christine! I feel as though you're putting me on the analyst's couch.'

Moving towards her, he took hold of both her hands.

'That wasn't my main reason for marrying you, and after all we've been through, I think it's time you trusted me.'

'Why should I do that?'

'Because I care about you, and listen to what you say. The trouble with you is, you listen but you don't hear. You look but you don't see.'

Her eyes darkened in confusion. 'I've both listened and looked, and I've tried to understand your motivation,' she said, 'but you're just a mass of contradictions.'

Palola's approach put paid to her train of thought.

'Fale all ready, very clean, I get help,' she said. 'Do not waste beautiful day. Where do you go?'

'We hadn't thought,' Adam replied, pleased that they could occupy their own house again. He turned to Christine. 'Did I tell you I've always been attracted to volcanoes?'

Christine laughed. 'I should think you act like one in the boardroom,' she quipped. 'What do you have in mind?'

'Tofua Island,' he replied. 'The famous mutiny on the Bounty took place near there. There's a beautiful crater lake and a very active volcano. If there's one place in Tonga that could blow my mind, that's it!'

'That's it then,' Christine echoed making her way towards the bridge. 'I'll go and change. How do we get there?'

'We can hitch a ride on one of the private fishing boats, or a launch, perhaps. Let's ask Palola to use coconut wireless and tell us when one of the boats is passing the island. Then we take a ride on one of the amphibian aircraft and land right on to the crater lake. Come on, Chris, let's go.'

Palola gave him one of her beaming smiles when he told her what they had in mind.

'You take food,' she said. 'Eat on beach and swim,' she said and hurried away to prepare a small picnic basket.

Wearing swimsuits under their clothes, Adam and Christine walked down to the lagoon where a small motor launch was already waiting to pick them up.

'We've done the trip several times,' Johnny, the owner of the launch, told them. 'It's fantastic, like something out of this world. After we've dropped you off, you fly in one of the lake amphibian aircraft. Believe me, it's an amazing experience. I take it you've never been to Tofua.'

'No, this is our first time,' Adam replied. 'We're on our honeymoon, actually, and we're really looking forward to seeing the crater and the volcano.'

'I'm glad to see you've brought your lunch,' the man went on, indicating the picnic basket. 'It could be difficult to obtain food on Tofua. There are only two small villages, and most inhabitants stay on the island part-time to harvest the kava crop.'

Once dropped off on the island, Adam and Christine found the owner of the amphibian aircraft and after a turbulent hop over the rim and a few tight passes around the sinister-looking volcano, it came to rest on the hauntingly-beautiful crater lake and taxied to the shore.

'I feel I've dropped into a lost world,' Adam said. 'I'm really impressed.' Then turning to Christine he went on, 'This trip was a good choice, don't you think? Just look at the colours in that lake. It really is amazing.'

'Did you say your name was Kyle?' the pilot said. 'Strange, that. It's not a common name and only a few days ago another Mrs Kyle and her companion came for the ride.'

Adam looked bemused. 'Another Mrs Kyle? There isn't . . . wait a minute. What did she look like?'

'Dishy,' he said, 'with beautiful long, black hair. Her boyfriend was older and fair-haired. They both said they had enjoyed the trip.'

'Are you absolutely sure her name was Kyle?' Adam said.

'Positive, but I can double-check if you like. I've got my appointment book back at the office.'

'No. No, I don't want to put you to any trouble,' Adam said, looking puzzled. 'I agree it's an uncommon name.'

Christine glanced at him, but he

clammed up about the other mysterious Mrs Kyle and was busy pressing the pilot for more information about the island. He told them that Tofua was ideal for camping, and there was plenty of scope for swimming, exploring the crater and its partially rainforested slopes and watching for rare birds.

'Sounds just up your alley,' Adam said to Christine with a grin. 'Pity we told that man with the launch that we'd be picked up at a certain time. We really need to stay longer, but we must fit in with his arrangements, of course.'

'Yes, he's been very kind.'

Christine stripped to her swimsuit and ran into the water.

'Come on, lazybones,' she called out to Adam. 'What are you waiting for?'

'Hey, you've forgotten my aching bones,' he said, running to join her.

They swam around, before throwing themselves down on the beach to dry out and enjoy the lunch Palola had prepared.

'This place is really something, isn't

it?' Adam said chewing on a leg of cooked chicken. 'We'll have to come again when we've got more time. We really needed to arrive much earlier in the day to make the most of it.'

He still hadn't mentioned the other Mrs Kyle again and with the experience of Tofua being so stimulating, she hesitated to bring up the subject.

'Now our swimsuits have dried out, I suppose we'd better make a move,' Adam said, picking up the clothes that he'd left in a heap on the sand. 'Can't keep Johnny waiting,' he went on, referring to the owner of the launch. 'His name is Johnny, isn't it?'

'Yes, it is, and I can't wait to tell him how much we enjoyed our trip,' Christine said. 'Who'd have thought such a sight existed. We've an awful lot to learn about the islands.'

The pilot of the aircraft flew them up and over the ridge then they walked to where the launch was waiting to pick them up.

'Well, what did you think?' Johnny

said, as they went on board. 'Did you fly right down into the crater?'

'We did, and, really, it's such an out-of-this-world experience, that I can hardly believe we've been there,' Christine told him.

'Let me offer you a drink,' Johnny said. 'I'm sure you must be ready for one after that walk to the boat. What shall it be?'

'Anything but kava,' Adam said with a grin. 'Kava just puts paid to the pair of us. We either get drunk or go to sleep. Have you any beer?'

'I've got lager, if that's any good,' and as they both nodded, he poured them a large glass each.

'If you've nothing else planned, you must go to the Ha'apai Festival,' Johnny said as they sipped their drinks. 'It's held in the first week in June. There's dancing, a beauty pageant to find Miss Ha'apai, and, oh, all manner of pageants, too numerous to mention.'

'How long does it last?' Christine asked.

'Three days,' Johnny replied. 'Last year, we had as much fun watching the crowds watch their friends, relatives and village leaders in the events, as we had in watching the events themselves.'

The time went very quickly as Johnny enthused about the festival and in what seemed like no time at all, they were being dropped off at their island.

'Nice chap, that Johnny,' Adam remarked as they walked through the clearing in the trees. 'Certainly made me want to go to that festival. We'll just drop the hamper off at Palola's house and then make our way to our own. I'll be glad to get back to a proper bed.'

He still hadn't said a word about Debra and questions were simmering on the tip of Christine's tongue. After she'd crossed the footbridge, she could contain her curiosity no longer.

'About that other mysterious Mrs Kyle,' she said. 'It was Debra, wasn't it?'

Adam opened the door and allowed her to pass through.

'Debra? How could it be? You're imagining things, just like that pilot. It must have been someone else. What would Debra be doing in the South Seas?'

'The same thing as us. She decided to take a holiday. She must have read about the Friendly Islands in a holiday brochure. Did you tell her where we were going on our honeymoon?'

She glanced at Adam out of the corner of her eye. She was very aware of how guarded he was, but she had to get to the bottom of it.

'I don't remember. I might have mentioned it. But even so . . .'

'Even so,' Christine finished for him, 'she knew where we were going, didn't she? Please answer my question, Adam. Did she know?'

'Not specifically,' he replied. 'She knew we were going to the South Seas but any number of people knew that.'

'Really, Adam, how can you be so naïve? She can't leave you alone, can she? Remember how she acted on our wedding day?'

'She was drunk.'

'That's not the point. It must have been Debra. Who else could it have been? She probably knows all about you, including your passion for volcanoes, so she'd guess where we were going, wouldn't she?'

'Well, I didn't make a secret of it, if that's what you mean.'

Adam paced up and down, obviously irritated by her questions.

'There were a dozen or more brochures lying around at Hunters' Lodge, so she probably . . . '

'Hunters' Lodge? What was she doing at Hunters' Lodge?'

'She was living there for a short time until the permanent housekeeper arrived.'

Christine felt rage sweep through her. This was the last straw! How dare he allow her to stay at Hunters' Lodge?

'But Hunters' Lodge was my family home, as well you know,' she said bitingly. 'When your company took it over I was forced to leave. Why was Debra allowed to stay? She had no claim on the company.'

'No, she didn't, but she offered to keep an eye on the place in the short term, and I thought it sensible to allow a member of the family to stay in residence until such time as . . . '

'Until such time as what?'

'I told you it was only temporary.'

'Why did you make a secret of it, Adam?'

'I didn't intend to keep it a secret. I just didn't happen to mention it. I intended to tell you about it before we went back to England.'

'Oh, I see. Well, thanks very much. That's very thoughtful of you.'

'Come on now, Chris. Even if it was Debra, and we've no proof that it was, why should it bother you? For all her past interest in me, she wouldn't dare try to find this island and interrupt our honeymoon. She was probably just intrigued by the literature on the crater and decided to take the trip. It was pure coincidence that it happened so close to our own trip. In any event, it seems she had a boyfriend with her.'

'I'm not so sure about that. She made it patently obvious that she wanted you for herself now that your brother's gone. I certainly wouldn't put her interest in you in the past tense.'

'Stop it, Christine!' Adam's patience was wearing thin.

Why should Debra's interest in Adam bother her anyway? Adam was her husband and Debra had no claim on him, and although she was married to Adam, it wasn't as if she loved him, so why was she being eaten up with jealousy? She thought for a moment. Was she being unjust to Debra? She didn't think so. It took a woman to see through the wiles of another, and where Debra was concerned, Adam was wearing a mask over his eyes.

'I'm going to bed,' Adam announced. 'I don't wish to continue this conversation. I suppose Palola has sorted out the sleeping arrangements. Tonight I need somewhere more comfortable to sleep.'

Christine stiffened with a renewed surge of anger. Despite what Adam had told her, the cold fingers of doubt were growing, spreading, icy tentacles reaching out to taint her marriage.

'I don't care where you sleep,' she spat out. 'As for me, I intend to sleep alone.'

And she turned away to hide the tears that were streaming, unheeded, down her cheeks.

7

Christine spent an uncomfortable night, tossing and turning in her sleep. She hadn't intended to sleep alone. She'd enjoyed her day on the volcanic island and she thought she and Adam had got on amazingly well, that is, until the subject of Debra raised its ugly head.

He seemed to be defending Debra and obviously thought a great deal about her, but the fact that she had been living at Hunters' Lodge was more than Christine could bear. She hadn't been consulted and knew that she would never have agreed to Debra living in the former family home, even if it was only for a limited amount of time.

Some of Christine's possessions were still there. The correspondence between herself and Jonathan Childes, for instance, was still locked in the bureau,

together with other important documents. At the time she'd thought it
preferable to lock them away at home
rather than trust them to a bank, but
now she wondered if she had made the
right decision.

After showering and donning her
swimsuit and the items of clothing
she'd worn the previous day, she
tip-toed past Adam's bedroom and
crept down the stairs. Once out of
the house, she walked slowly along the
sandy beach.

Maybe a swim would rid her of her
blue mood, she thought as she plunged
into the water. She felt light as air,
forgetting for the moment any worries
on her mind when suddenly and
without warning she felt a sharp stab of
pain.

'Ouch,' she exclaimed, and the colour
fled from her cheeks when she saw the
water tinged red with her own blood.

Hopping on one foot until she
reached the beach, she lay down and
examined her foot. It was a really nasty

gash. She couldn't stem the flow of blood and being on her own, panic engulfed her. What was she going to do?

Next minute, she found herself being hoisted up into a pair of strong, brown arms. Katanga, the fisherman they had seen before on the reef, had seen her. He'd realised what had happened and had come swiftly to her aid. Smiling to reassure her, he made giant strides towards Palola's house. The native woman threw up her hands in horror when she saw the blood still pouring from Christine's foot. She clicked her fingers and immediately two islanders appeared. She said something to them in her own language and they quickly reappeared carrying a frond mattress. Carefully, Christine was placed upon it.

'You need doctor. We take to husband now,' Palola said and they crossed over the footbridge where Adam came to meet them.

'Good heavens! What happened to you?' he asked in an anxious voice. 'That looks bad. Better clean it up and get a bandage on it. Is it hurting much?'

'Yes, it is,' Christine said. 'I cut it on a reef. Perhaps we ought to bathe it with some antiseptic. Ouch, the pain is killing me.'

'You go see doctor. Foot plenty bad,' Palola said. 'Coconut wireless say boat come soon. You go now.'

'Yes. I'll just cleanse the wound and put a bandage on it,' Adam said, and when he had done so and bathed it with some antiseptic, which made Christine cry out loud, he lifted her back on to the frond mattress and they all went down to the lagoon to wait for the ferry.

'What happened to your foot?' the ferry-master asked.

'I was swimming and cut it on coral,' Christine said. 'It's stopped bleeding now, thank goodness. Palola thinks we ought to see a doctor.'

'Yes, she's quite right. There's a pharmacy in the clinic at Nuku'alofa, but they wouldn't be able to give you an antibiotic injection. Better for you to go to the private practice. There's a German doctor there. She may be able to see you when she sees what state you're in.'

'Thanks,' Christine said. 'We'll try there then. We can take a taxi from the docks. I don't feel like walking too far.'

Fortunately the lady doctor was free and they were ushered into her surgery.

'You did the right thing coming to see me,' she said. 'It's a really nasty gash. The moist, warm conditions mean that even a small cut or scratch can become painfully infected, and lead to more serious problems. I'll give you an antibiotic injection, a course of tablets and some antiseptic cream. Come back in a week's time for a check-up. It should have healed by then.'

'Thank you, you're very kind,' Christine said. 'I'm grateful you fitted me in.'

'Before you go, I'll need to make out a record card,' the doctor said. 'I'll need your name and address.'

'My name's Christine Kyle. My

home address is . . .'

She hestitated for a moment and Adam finished for her.

'Hunters' Lodge, Bedfordshire, U.K.'

'Kyle?' the doctor said. 'KYLE — is that how you spell it?'

'Yes, that's right,' Christine replied. 'Well, thanks again.'

Adam paid the doctor's fee and they walked out into the sunshine, Adam holding Christine up as she hobbled on one leg.

'I know what you're thinking,' Adam remarked as they hailed a taxi to take them back to the ferry. 'You were thinking she was going to say Kyle was an uncommon name, or something of that ilk now, weren't you?'

'Well, I suppose it is an uncommon name now I come to think about it. But she didn't say so, did she, so there's no point in our discussing it.'

It was still early in the day when they arrived back at the island.

'Now you keep quiet and put your foot up on this settee,' Adam said. 'Will you be all right on your own for a while? I thought I might make some more notes if necessary, take some more photographs. There are some books over there you may care to read, so you won't get bored. Shan't be long.'

She tried to sleep once he'd gone but sleep just wouldn't come, so she looked for the books Adam had told her about. She could see a pile of them on the other side of the room with a stack of files on top. That meant she'd have to move from the settee. She got up slowly and hobbled round, but when she tried to get one of the books out of the pile, one of Adam's files fell on to the floor, the contents spewing all over the place.

Managing to bend down and pick them up, she realised they were print-outs of e-mails sent to Adam from his Los Angeles office. Carefully she put them into date order only pausing to glance at the one on the top. She hadn't intended to read it, but when Debra's name sprang out at her, the temptation was too great.

Senior positions filled as instructed. Vacancy still to be filled for Administrator's Secretary. Have received an application from Debra Kyle but no CV was included. As she is your sister-in-law, wanted to advise you before taking any action. Will await your instructions.

Still reeling from the recent knowledge that Debra had been living at Hunters' Lodge, Christine couldn't believe what she'd read. How typical of Debra. She was trying every angle. Furious at the thought of her working for the former Bradleys House of Antiques, she almost flung the e-mail across the room, but when she had calmed down she had second thoughts about it.

The office would have expected a reply. Had Adam sent one yet? Carefully, she switched on his lap-top and checked. No, as far as she could make out, there was no item listed under his sent messages, and nothing in the outbox, so he must still be thinking about how to reply.

Still angry with Debra for trying to wangle her way into the firm, Christine suddenly had an idea. She would send a message herself and pretend it came from Adam, nothing too detrimental, just to keep the thing on ice. But what could she say? She thought for a moment before she clicked on to New Mail then she typed in the office e-mail address, subject, Debra Kyle.

Thank your for your e-mail, she typed. Suggest you set up interviews with other likely candidates for secretary's job. Please hold Debra Kyle's application for the time being and keep me in the picture. Will then give further instructions.

As soon as she'd typed it she regretted it. What was she doing? She had no right to interfere, no right to read his e-mails. Adam would be furious with her if he found out about it. She felt ashamed, stupid and sick with regret.

Get rid of it at once, she told herself, but the sound of voices approaching threw her off guard. Instead of clicking the **Delete** button she clicked on the **Save and Send Later** icon, and with no time to rectify her mistake, she logged off and stumbled back to the settee.

Adam and Palola walked in, accompanied by a gang of laughing island young girls who placed a lei round Christine's neck, then ran giggling out of the house.

'Girls bring lei to make you smile,' Palola said. 'Later I bring food.'

'Yes, what do you fancy?' Adam asked.

'I haven't really much of an appetite. Perhaps it's the injection and the pills,' she replied.

Knowing she hadn't got rid of that e-mail had made her anxious and completely wrecked her appetite.

'What about some fish?' Adam said. 'Fish should go down OK.'

Christine nodded her agreement. If she refused to eat, Adam would suspect something was wrong.

'Yes, that's a good idea,' she replied. 'Fish will be fine.'

'I bring fish, yes?' Palola asked, crossing to the door.

'That's settled then.' Adam reached for a glass of coconut milk. 'Care for some of this? Those girls were shaking the trunk of a palm tree to bring the coconuts down and one of them narrowly missed my head! Did you manage to get through those guide books then?'

Christine shook her head.

'Never mind. While Palola prepares our meal, I'll give you a quick rundown of what's on offer.'

Picking up one of the glossy pamphlets he went on, 'There's so much to see and do. I hardly know where to begin. Bush walking.'

He stopped and glanced at Christine's foot.

'No, you're not ready for that yet. Snorkelling and diving — that's more in my line. And how about the flying foxes?' His eyes twinkled. 'How would they suit an environmentalist? But wait a minute, they're not foxes, they're bats.'

'Bats? Ugh! I don't fancy them,' Christine interjected.

'And they've got a terrific wing span,' Adam went on. 'They literally hang about in the trees — spooky! And if you've had no luck spotting the Red Shining Parrot,' he said, turning a page, 'here's your chance to see what you've missed.'

Christine couldn't help but laugh.

'Go on, you're pulling my leg.'

'No, really. You just need to visit the Brehm Bird Park. Well, at least that's put a smile on your face.'

'I'm sorry. I'm still feeling under the weather. What does it say about the Tongan National Centre?'

'Just a minute, let me find the right page. Oh, here it is. It says it was established to promote conservation awareness. There you are, girl, your two favourite words. It's really worth a visit. There's lectures, handicrafts, weaving, jewellery and fashion parades — just up your street.'

He went on talking about the other attractions, and Christine realised she'd never asked him about his day.

'Nothing spectacular,' he said. 'I've taken some more photographs, and I've got a wad of notes. Sometime when I get round to it, I'll have to get them on the word processor.'

At the mention of that word, Christine froze. When he switched on his lap-top he'd be bound to check for e-mails and the computer would tell him he had one saved message, awaiting the instruction either to go on line or send it now.

And when he'd read it, what then? What would he say? It didn't bear thinking about. She felt so guilty. He'd been so kind and patient, trying to entertain her with all the sights they could visit together once her foot had healed. But if he refused to go without her, what chance did she have of deleting the e-mail now?

A light tap on the door interrupted her gloomy thoughts. The food had arrived. She didn't think she was hungry, but the freshly-caught fish tasted so good she ate with good appetite. When the remains of their meal had been taken away and she had taken the tablets the doctor had prescribed, she fought to stay awake, but found herself drifting off into sleep.

Not wanting to disturb her, Adam kissed the tip of her nose, covered her with a length of woven fabric, and tip-toed out of the room.

8

They stayed close to home for the next few days while Christine's foot healed, lying in their hammocks, enjoying the perfect weather and Palola's culinary skills. At bedtime, Adam insisted on sleeping alone and Christine had been surprised by not enjoying the seclusion of a solitary bed. She missed the comfort of his arms around her, the sense of security she felt from his closeness.

The more she thought about the e-mail, the more she chided herself. She dreaded to think what his reaction would be when he found out, as he was bound to do. Would he lose his cool and call her an interfering nuisance? She knew she deserved no less, but she was not a coward and she knew she would face up to it despite the recriminations.

Each day, her foot improved a little

and soon it had healed completely.

'How's the foot?' Adam asked when he saw she was walking normally. 'Let me take a look at it.'

She held it up for his inspection, and he placed an arm around her waist to support her.

'Looks all right to me,' he said, releasing her, 'but I think you should visit that doctor again now that you've finished your course of tablets, just to be on the safe side.'

Christine agreed. 'Yes, that's my intention. I'll find out when there's a ferry.'

Adam stretched his arms above his head in a playful, lazy gesture.

'I'm getting lazy,' he said. 'If you're going to be tied up with the doctors this might be as good a time as any for me to go island hopping. I want to sound out that English banana plantation owner, Jack Hargreaves, get his opinion as to whether or not he thinks a development here would be a financial disaster.'

'An environmental disaster more like,' Christine retorted, 'but sound him out by all means. I'll definitely go and see that doctor for a check-up,' she went on. 'Then I'll take a look round the Tongan Trade Centre. From what you've told me, it's well worth a visit.'

She went off to change, then returned to pick up her bag ready to leave.

'Mind how you go,' Adam called after her.

The weather was fabulous as she eventually walked from the docks to the nearest telephone. She asked if the doctor could see her, but was told the lady doctor she had seen the previous week was on holiday, but a male Tongan doctor would see her in a couple of hours.

That gave her plenty of time to go to the Tongan Trade Centre and see what was on offer. After asking the way, she took the bus from town and got off at the Centre. It turned out to be a vast cultural centre and there was so much going on that at first, Christine was fazed by it all.

The receptionist handed her a brochure which listed all the events, and she had a quick look through it. Apparently Tongan handicrafts were the most beautiful and affordable in the Pacific, and Christine couldn't wait to look round. The magnificent black pearls, locked away in a glass case, were so enormously expensive that no price tag had to be shown. They had a superb lustre and she was awestruck gazing at them, but she had to buy something, and she indulged herself by buying a black coral necklace and matching bracelet, both of which she couldn't resist.

She checked on how much money she had left. Better stop buying and put the rest of her cash towards the doctor's fee, she thought, and headed off to the surgery. The male Tongan doctor asked her name and sent for her record card.

'Mrs Kyle?' he enquired. 'Oh, yes, you were here last week when you saw my lady colleague. How do you like Tonga?'

'Very much,' Christine replied. 'I've just come back from the National Trade Centre. It was fascinating, but with so many visitors around it got rather hot in there, despite the air conditioning.'

'Well, you want to take care in these early months,' the doctor said, consulting his record card. 'Anything can happen and you're a long way from home.'

He glanced at the record card again.

'I hope you're taking the extra calcium and the vitamin pills.'

What was he talking about?

'Yes,' he went on, before she could reply, 'in your condition it's advisable to take them regularly. Now correct me if I'm wrong, but according to my records, you're in your sixth week of pregnancy. Is that right?'

Stunned, Christine didn't hear the rest of what he was saying. What did he mean? He'd obviously made a mistake.

'No, you don't understand,' Christine

explained. 'I'm not pregnant. As a matter of fact, I've only recently been married. You must be confusing me with someone else.'

'Well, let me see.' The doctor held the card up towards the light. 'Are you Mrs Kyle of Hunters' Lodge, Bedfordshire, England?'

'Yes, but . . . '

'Mrs Debra Kyle?'

Christine drew in a breath, and a small, cold shiver sneaked down the length of her spine. Debra? Was she here? Was she pregnant? By whom? She hastened to correct the doctor.

'No, you've confused me with another Mrs Kyle. Debra Kyle is my husband's sister-in-law. I'm Mrs Adam Kyle and my christian name is Christine. I came in with an injured foot and was given an injection and some antibiotics.'

She tried to speak calmly, but her heart was pounding against her ribs.

'So if you'll just check my foot, I won't take up any more of your time.'

The doctor apologised profusely.

'I'm very sorry, Mrs Kyle. I've been given the wrong card. Oh, yes, now let me see,' he went on once he'd been given the correct card. 'You cut your foot on a coral reef. How does it feel now?'

Still reeling from what she had been told, she held up her foot for the doctor to examine.

'It seems to have healed very well,' he said. 'Any bad reaction or allergies?'

'No, nothing at all. It's fine really. I thought I'd just pop in and get it checked. But obviously there's no need for me to come again.'

'No, it's fine, and I do apologise for the mix-up.' He smiled. 'Good job it was someone in the family. Matter of confidentiality, you know. Perhaps you'd better keep it to yourself for the time being. Wait for Mrs Kyle to tell you herself. At the proper time she'll be only too delighted to tell you, I'm sure. Perhaps she wants it to be a surprise.'

'Yes, well, I won't say a word,' Christine said as she tried to gather her wits together.

After paying the doctor's fee, she hurried out into the street. No matter what the doctor had confided in her, Adam must be told, and sooner rather than later. Debra was clearly among the islands. As she hurried back to the docks, she tried to figure out the best way to tell him. No point in wrapping it up or trying to conceal it in any way. No, she would tell him straight out, everything the doctor had told her.

When she was dropped off at the island, all her old fears came flooding back. She was more convinced than ever that Debra was following Adam around, but what did she hope to gain by it? And who was the father of her child? Was it the man the pilot had told them about who'd accompanied her to the crater?

Question was heaped upon question. How would Adam react when she told him? Knowing how she felt about Debra, he'd probably accuse her of making it up, but it was there, in black and white on a medical card, and there was no denying it.

She ran along the beach accompanied by the island look-out who had been watching from the top of a palm tree. Palola came to meet her and stopped her in her tracks. The native woman was naturally anxious that her doctor's report had gone well, so it would be rude and inconsiderate to ignore her.

'What did doctor say?' Palola asked. 'Did she say foot was well?'

'Yes, yes, my foot is fine, thank you. I must go and find Adam and tell him the good news.'

'Yes, you tell,' Palola called out after her. 'Husband be pleased. All island pleased. You have guest. I cook for you.'

Christine ran across the wooden bridge filled with trepidation. Palola must have made a mistake. Neither she nor Adam was expecting anyone, but as she approached the house, she could make out two figures relaxing on the veranda, and unless she was very much mistaken, one of them was a woman!

9

As she approached, she saw Adam lying in one of the hammocks, talking in an animated way to a tanned, young woman who was lying in the other hammock, and whose tawny curtain of hair swung below her waist. On seeing Christine, they both stood up and moved towards her.

Christine quickly appraised the girl. Who was she? With a visitor around, she wouldn't be able to tell Adam about Debra. It was simmering on the tip of her tongue, but now it would have to be put on hold.

The girl was in her mid-twenties, Christine supposed. Adam came forward.

'Chris, this is Laura Hargreaves, Jack Hargreaves' daughter. If you recall, I went to see him this morning. Laura, Christine, my wife.'

'Hi!'

Laura smiled and extended her hand.

'It's lovely to meet you, Christine. I don't wonder you look surprised. I bet you wondered who the heck it was keeping your husband company.'

Christine returned her smile. The girl seemed friendly enough and she took to her right away although she'd no idea why she was here.

'Laura works for her father,' Adam explained. 'She was born in England but she's spent most of her life in New Zealand.'

'Yes, that's true,' Laura confirmed. 'I fell in love with New Zealand but that was before I came to stay with Dad. It's quite easy to get to Tonga from New Zealand, and I come and go like a yo-yo. As you know, Dad grows and exports bananas. He oversees the growing and packing and I look after the paperwork and administration.'

She must have a very responsible job, Christine thought, she's an interesting person as well. For all her good intentions, Palola couldn't really hold a conversation, and Christine sometimes longed for another female to chat to. Girl talk, that's what she missed. She supposed Adam wanted to get Laura's opinion of the island. Without any axe to grind, Christine knew it would be completely unbiased and all the more valuable for that.

'Well, if we can persuade you to stay for dinner, I promise we won't offer you bananas,' Christine said.

'She's doing better than that,' Adam said. 'Jack's too busy to give any time to coming over here, so he sent his daughter instead. I suggested she start her tour in the morning as she's agreed to stay the night. That's all right with you, Chris, isn't it?'

'Yes, of course it is.'

While Adam was looking for an outside opinion on the future good of the islands, there might still be some hope, Christine thought to herself. If she could persuade Laura to take a similar stance to herself once she'd explored the island, Adam might be more inclined to give the development a thumbs down. It was worth a try.

'Thanks very much,' Laura said, turning to Christine. 'I'd love to stay if it isn't too much trouble.'

'Here, give me your overnight bag and I'll take it upstairs while you two have a natter,' Adam said.

Laura handed it over.

'I feel rather guilty interrupting your honeymoon,' Laura said, smiling at Christine. 'I don't want to intrude. Adam's very anxious to get a second opinion of any future development of this island, isn't he?' she went on. 'My father was really the person to come over. I know nothing about development or property deals, so why . . . '

'That's why,' Christine explained. 'He's looking for a completely unbiased view. He wants to know if the other plantation owners would think housing on this island would be a good idea or would they dismiss it out of hand.'

'I see what you mean. He's some

kind of entrepreneur, isn't he?'

'A term that covers a multitude of sins,' Christine retorted sharply.

Laura laughed. 'I take it you don't approve.'

'I have to tell you that personally I'm dead against it,' Christine said. 'The island's completely unspoiled, and the islanders want to keep it that way. Once you've had a chance to look round, I'm sure you'll agree with me.'

'Agree with you about what?' Adam said, entering the room.

'Oh, nothing for you to worry about,' Christine said. 'We were discussing Palola and her cooking methods. Her speciality is corned beef cooked in coconut cream.'

'Corned beef, a speciality? You must be joking.'

'No, really. You'd hardly recognise it as being ordinary corned beef after they've finished with it. There's plenty to drink, too, but Adam and I keep off kava!'

'I don't blame you. Our packers

drink it, but Dad and I can't take it. It's lethal.' Laura looked thoughtful. 'The kava plantation owners don't agree with us, though. Kava's a very popular drink throughout the islands. They introduce it to the tourists and make a mint out of it.'

'Yes, I suppose they do,' Adam said. 'When Chris and I tried it, it knocked us for six. Going back to the development for a moment, I wonder if the kava plantation owners would be interested in the type of housing I have in mind, as well as the banana plantation owners, I mean. If the scheme came to fruition, that is. Perhaps . . . '

'Now come on, Adam, we're not discussing business tonight,' Christine interrupted quickly. 'This is a social occasion, and I can hear voices, and the strumming of guitars. Looks as though our dinner has arrived.'

Walking out into the bright sunlight, the three of them saw several islanders carrying food on lengths of frond, with Palola at the head giving instructions, while other islanders serenaded Christine and Laura.

With Laura here, I've just got to try to relax and enjoy myself, Christine thought. I'll just have to wait until the time is right to tell Adam about Debra, but it's difficult for me to keep the lid on it. Damn Debra! What on earth was she playing at?

'Christine come back to us.' Adam's voice drew her out of her reverie. 'You look very serious. What are you thinking about?'

'Oh, nothing,' Christine replied hastily. 'I was concentrating on these fabulous dishes Palola has brought. I don't know what to choose.'

'Neither do I,' Laura said with a grin. 'They all look so appetising.'

They finally decided on a bit of this and a bit of that.

'I couldn't eat another thing,' Laura said later. 'It's lovely to be serenaded while you eat. It's never happened to me before. I've never seen anything like it.'

'By the way, Chris. You haven't told

us how you enjoyed your visit to the Trade Centre,' Adam said. 'And did you see the doctor about your foot? Did she say you needed any more treatment?'

'No, and it wasn't a her it was a him,' Chris replied. 'He examined my foot and told me it was just fine.'

This wasn't the time to tell Adam what she'd learned about Debra, not with Laura sitting right next to them.

'Tell me about the Trade Centre. What did you buy?' Adam said, changing the subject, to Christine's relief.

'Excuse me a moment and I'll show you.'

Running back into the house, she found the black coral necklace and bracelet she had bought and put them on.

'They're lovely,' Laura said as Christine showed them off. 'I've been to the centre several times. It's an amazing place. Did you see the black pearls?'

'Yes, they're fabulous. You should

have seen them,' Christine said to Adam.

'Fabulously expensive, too,' Laura said. 'That's why they're locked away.'

'There were so many other things, too,' Christine said. 'Oh, look, Palola's beckoning to us to follow her. Looks like the dancing's about to begin.'

The three of them joined the circle of islanders who were squatting on the ground.

'This is really exciting,' Laura said, as the girls began to dance. 'Dad doesn't know what he's missing, and if David saw these dusky maidens he'd be in his element.'

Christine sat up, interested.

'David?'

'He's my brother,' Laura replied. 'Dad always wanted him to work on the plantation, but David had other ideas. He wanders all over New Zealand buying and selling things, or rather that is what he'd have us believe. He's a law unto himself. We never really know what he does for a living, but he's got good looks and charm, so whatever trouble he may get into, he always manages to wriggle out of it.'

Christine looked puzzled.

'You mean . . . '

'Customs and Excise, that sort of thing. But whenever he feels he wants to get away from it all, he comes back to the islands for some peace and quiet. We're expecting a visit from him anytime now. He's coming over to the island, with his pregnant girlfriend in tow. She's only in the early stages, but she insists the baby's David's and is clinging to him like a leech. We've never met her. In fact, we don't even know her name, but with a bit of luck they'll arrive in time for the Ha'apai festival. It lasts for three days, you know, and it's not to be missed.'

'Yes, we've heard about it,' Adam said. 'It seems well worth a visit.'

'It is,' Laura said, 'and David will love it. As well as his shady dealings, he's an experienced diver and snorkeller, so he'll never be short of cash. I don't know about his girlfriend though,' she went on. 'When David goes off on a frolic of his own you can never be quite sure when he's coming back, so she may have to latch on to us for a while.'

What a strange way to behave, Christine thought, wondering what kind of girl would put up with that. In the early stages of pregnancy, Laura had said. What a coincidence! Debra was six weeks pregnant according to the doctor. Surely there couldn't be any connection. No, she was just letting her imagination run riot. What possible interest could Debra have in Laura's brother?

Nevertheless, she was anxious to tell Adam about Debra's visit to the doctor and now that Laura was dancing with one of the islanders, she tried to bring the subject up, but Adam would have none of it.

'No, I don't want to discuss Debra when we're all having such fun,' he protested. 'What do you think of Laura?

I did the right thing, didn't I, asking her to stay?'

'Of course. She's a very friendly person. I took to her right away.'

Christine watched the girl trying her best to keep up with the swaying islanders.

'And she certainly seems fit. Don't know what to make of her brother though. He's an experienced snorkeller and diver, but from what she said, he seems to prefer the life of a reprobate. What's the father like?'

'Jack? He's a hard-headed business-man, but you have to be if you want to run a successful outfit like his. He dotes on Laura. He told me a more supportive daughter would be hard to find. He hopes she'll find someone to marry one day, but her standards are very high. Not that she's likely to find a husband on that banana plantation. Strangely enough, he never mentioned he had a son. The first I knew of it was when Laura mentioned it just now.'

'That's because he probably doesn't

approve of him,' Christine replied, but knowing she had to tread carefully, she went on, 'and David's girlfriend. What do you make of her?'

Before he could reply, a flushed Laura flung herself down beside them.

'Phew!' she exclaimed. 'You need some energy to keep up with them. Give me a drink, quick.'

'I've asked Palola if we can borrow her cousin's horses tomorrow, so we can explore the island,' Adam said. 'You haven't much time, have you, before you have to go back?'

'Regretfully, no,' Laura replied. 'With new orders coming in every day, it's heaven help me if I don't keep abreast of things.' She laughed. 'Dad can be a hard taskmaster, but he knows the score.' She stifled a yawn. 'Oh, sorry, excuse me. All that exertion's catching up with me. Don't think I'm being rude, but what time do you intend to turn in?'

'Anytime now,' Christine said. 'We've got a long day ahead of us tomorrow if you're to see everything there is to see. What time are you expecting to leave?'

'On the late afternoon ferry,' Laura replied. 'Coconut wireless will let us know if it's going to be late. It's weird, isn't it? No-one can explain it, but it always seems to work.'

She glanced around.

'It'll be hard to leave this place though. The music and the dancing have really got to me, not to mention the food.'

'Yes, London is a long way from our thoughts, isn't it, Chris?' Adam said. 'Oh, well, who's for bed? Christine, how about you?'

'Yes, I'm really tired,' Christine replied. 'Come on, Laura, let's take you back to our house.'

Laura went up to her room and was quickly followed by Christine and Adam.

'Adam, there's something I've got to tell you,' Christine said when they were alone. 'It's about Debra and . . . '

'Well, I'm sure it will keep, whatever

it is. I'm too sleepy to talk about it now.'

'No, you don't understand. It won't keep. It's something that the doctor told me. Please, Adam, you've got to listen!'

Her voice had reached a high crescendo.

'Stop talking that way, and keep a hold on yourself,' he muttered. 'Laura's in the next room. She'll hear you and wonder what I've done to upset you.'

'You haven't done anything. It isn't you. That's what I'm trying to say. It was the doctor, he said . . .'

She was still getting no response from Adam.

'I'm going to take a shower,' he said. 'I suggest you do the same. It might help clear your head.'

'No, not tonight. I'm sleepy and it's late.'

Only it wasn't true. She knew she would find it hard to sleep with thoughts of Debra on her mind. Taking off her necklace and bracelet, she walked over to the window and glanced out into the lush darkness.

With Laura in the picture, Adam had made no effort to work on his computer, but Christine knew that if she touched his lap-top again, he might walk in on her and ask her what she was doing. Every time she thought about it, she quaked inside. It was only a matter of time before he checked his e-mails and realised what she'd done.

How would he react?

She knew the answer only too well, and her head ached as she went to bed and eventually fell into a troubled sleep.

10

Next morning, the weather was perfect, with a promise of soaring temperatures tempered by a slight breeze. Adam was busily sorting out the various breakfast dishes that Palola had brought sometime earlier when Christine entered the room.

'There's plenty to choose from here,' he said, eyeing the various bowls of exotic fruits and juice. 'Have you seen Laura this morning?'

Laura heard him as she came running down the stairs.

'I'm here,' she replied, viewing the dishes on offer. 'May I help myself to some of that delicious mango?'

'Of course. Choose anything you like,' Christine said. 'It's difficult to decide, isn't it? I've had that problem ever since we came here. Palola will also have prepared a picnic lunch for us,' she went on. 'We'll collect it when we pick up the horses. One of her cousins owns them and they're very gentle and well-behaved.'

'Now what am I going to need?' Adam said. 'My clipboard, various rough plans and a video camera. My notes are in a bit of a tangle. If you'll wait for thirty minutes or so, Laura, I'll bring them up to date on my word processor and . . . '

'No, don't bother,' Laura said. 'You can type them out later and fax them to Dad. They won't mean all that much to me, you know.'

'OK,' Adam said. 'If you've both finished your breakfast, we'll be on our way. We're picking up the horses at Palola's house, Laura. It will save them being brought across the wooden footbridge.'

'Right,' Laura said, making for the door. 'I'm looking forward to this.'

They breathed in the blossom-scent as the crossed the footbridge. As promised, three tame-looking horses were tethered to Palola's veranda.

'You go explore the island,' Palola said with one of her beaming smiles. 'Horses all ready. Picnic ready, too. Coconut wireless give time of ferry so welcome visitor can go back to island. Sorry when visitor goes. You come back soon,' she said to Laura.

'She's wonderful, isn't she?' Laura said, as they mounted the three chestnut mares and Adam hoisted up the picnic basket. 'Where do we start?'

Adam instructed his horse to walk on and the girls followed close behind, the horses nuzzling each other as they made their way through the sheltering palms. When they reached a clearing which led on to the white sandy beach, Adam dismounted and pointed up to a high reef where Katanga was casting his line.

'Do you see him, Laura?' he enquired, unfolding his plans. 'Just look up there on the high reef. That's Katanga, the icon of our fishing industry. He caught the fish you ate last night.'

He pointed to the site on his plan.

'Trouble is, that will be a prime site if we go ahead with the development, so we'll have to move him out of the way.'

He shielded his eyes from the glaring sun.

'Just look at that view! Just think what someone would pay for that!'

'It's quite amazing,' Laura said, dismounting. 'Don't you think so, Chris? He knows he's in a very good position, fishing from up there. I shouldn't think he'd take kindly to being moved.'

'His personal feelings don't come into the equation, Laura,' Adam said in a tone of dry cynicism. 'As I said to your father, I never let personal feelings interfere with business. If you're all set on making a profit, they don't count.'

He walked along the sand, punching out his points.

'Sorry, but where business is concerned, that's just the way things are.'

Christine and Laura exchanged glances

behind his back.

'Now you see the strength of the opposition,' Christine whispered to Laura. 'Come on, Adam, show Laura where some of the other sites are.'

Tethering their horses to a palm tree, the three of them walked on for a while, Adam stopping now and again to point out future sites while Laura took some photographs.

Soon it was time to refresh themselves and, walking back to where they had left the horses, Adam reached for the picnic basket. They sat down in the shade of a great banyan tree. Opening the hamper, Adam poured drinks for them all.

'How long do you intend to stay on the island?' Laura enquired.

'We haven't decided yet, have we, Chris?' Adam replied. 'We're not only on honeymoon but combining it with business. I won't feel guilty if we stay say, another two weeks at least. There's still so much to see.'

'You mean you're on business,'

Christine remarked wryly. 'As for me, I'm just here for the ride. But Adam's right, you know. There's so much we haven't seen yet.'

'Have you been to the flying fox colony?' Laura asked. 'If not, it's well worth a visit. It's only eleven miles from Nuku'alofa.'

'No. Adam mentioned it, but I didn't fancy it,' Christine said. 'They're not foxes, they're bats. And I don't like bats.'

'Well, they're not like Dracula, if that's what you're thinking.' Laura laughed. 'They're quite interesting really. Legend has it that they were a love gift from Hina, a Samoan maiden, to one of the ancient chiefs. The Friendly Islands are all about love. I thought perhaps that's why you chose one of them for your honeymoon.'

'Well, we couldn't have made a better choice, could we?' Christine said. 'The island's completely unspoiled, as you can see. I can't bear to think of it being commercialised with hot-dog stands, fish and chips and towering hotel blocks.'

'I've already told you a hundred times it wouldn't be like that.'

Christine could see that Adam was losing his cool.

'There's still so many problems to be solved. The necessity of an airstrip for one, and that's only the beginning. As Laura knows, it's not possible to buy the land. It all belongs to the Tongan Government. That means long, protracted negotiations for a long lease. Then there's the question of planning permission. These are issues that cannot be solved overnight.'

'I know what you mean,' Laura replied. 'No need to lose your cool, but having seen part of the island, I can well understand Christine's reservations about developing it.'

'Well, you're both entitled to your point of view,' Adam replied, pouring himself a drink. 'I agree that it needs a lot of careful thought.'

Glancing in Laura's direction, he

raised one eyebrow quizzically.

'I needed an unbiased opinion and now it seems I've got one.'

'Don't take any notice of me,' Laura said. 'I'm afraid I use my heart, not my head. Dad may take the opposite view. If you do your notes and fax them over, he'll have his own opinion, I'm sure.'

'Come on, Adam, don't get all steamed up about it,' Christine said. 'Up until now, it's two against one, but neither of us is professional so . . . '

'I'm sorry. I didn't mean to put a damper on things,' Adam said, then turning to Laura he added, 'I'm really grateful you've given us so much of your time. I know you'll have to get back soon, so let's finish our tour of the island and forget about the business for a while. There's a spectacular coral reef I really want you to see.'

Later, Laura said her goodbye to Palola and was rewarded with a big hug. Then Adam and Christine walked down to the lagoon where the ferry was waiting to take Laura back to her father.

'Don't forget the Ha'apai Festival's next week,' Laura called to them as they waved her off. 'There's nothing to compare with it. We must meet up. It's a fantastic experience. Let me know which day you'll be going.'

Christine mouthed, 'Yes,' then she and Adam turned and walked back to the house.

'Now Laura's gone, I need to check with my management team,' Adam said, 'and there's all these notes on the island that need typing up. Can you amuse yourself for an hour or two while I get on with it?'

Christine shot him a nervous look before he strode away. She still hadn't told him about Debra, and when he switched on his lap-top he'd find the saved but unsent e-mail and all mayhem would break loose.

Moving over to the bar, she poured herself a stiff drink, but it didn't seem to help. Escape was impossible. She was a sitting duck, and she felt as though she were sitting on a time-bomb that would explode at any moment.

Pacing up and down the veranda, she heard a loud exclamation as Adam appeared carrying a sheaf of e-mails.

'What the devil's all this about?' he fumed, thrusting the offending e-mail under Christine's nose. 'What are you playing at, Chris? You were going to send this, weren't you? Thank goodness I caught it in time.'

Christine had never seen him so angry and involuntarily she cowered away as he towered over her.

'Is this what you've been trying to tell me about Debra?'

Sick with self disgust, Christine did her utmost to explain.

'Yes, but that isn't the only thing. There's more. You see . . . '

'More? What do you mean, more? Did you ring my office and tell them you had a message from me saying they were not to employ Debra at any price? Or maybe that wasn't enough.'

'No. No, please, don't go on so. Don't be sarcastic, Adam, please. Just let me explain. Just listen for a moment.' Her voice was tense and nervous. 'You see, I knocked over your file quite by accident, your file with the e-mails in it and I saw the one about Debra applying for a job with my father's firm.'

'Your father's firm? It is no longer your father's firm.' Adam was clearly enraged.

'No, well, I know that, but it was just the thought of her working there. I couldn't bear it. It worried me and . . . '

'Worried you? You would have had more to worry about if you'd sent that e-mail to my management team. Whatever were you thinking of?'

'I don't know. Something came over me. I was confused when I saw Debra's name. I hated myself after I'd typed it and was going to delete it, then I heard you coming and I panicked and clicked on to save instead of deleting it.'

Christine hardly paused for breath.

'I'm sorry, Adam. It was confidential information. There's no excuse. I had no right.'

'I see.' His voice sounded strained and distant. 'And what else is it you were longing to tell me? More forays into my private correspondence?'

'No. Really, Adam, I never meant to pry, and I won't ever do it again, I promise. But, yes, there is something else. Listen, please. I know you won't believe me, but it must have been Debra who visited the volcano that day because . . . '

'Stop it, Christine! You've got Debra on the brain. I refuse to listen to any more of your infantile ranting.'

'No, it's true, and I can prove it.' Christine struggled to keep her voice on an even keel. 'You remember that I went to the doctor for a check-up? He was given my record card you see, only it wasn't my record card and . . . '

'Christine, you're not making sense. Was it your card or wasn't it?'

'I'm trying to tell you, if you'll only

listen.' Christine moved forward, determined to stand her ground. 'The receptionist gave the doctor the record card for another Mrs Kyle by mistake, a Mrs Debra Kyle, who went for a check-up because she was six weeks pregnant. Debra is following us, Adam, or rather she's following you. I don't know why, especially now she's pregnant, and there's more. You remember what Laura told us about her brother, David, and a woman six weeks pregnant who has latched on to him?'

'Oh, for goodness' sake, Christine, stop acting like a spoiled brat and control yourself. Now you're trying to say David's the father of Debra's baby?'

'Well, he could be.'

'You're lying, Christine.'

'I'm not.' Christine fought for control. 'Of course, it needn't be David, it could be someone else, but . . . '

'You're making this up. This whole thing about Debra makes me feel sick.'

Adam stopped speaking and poured himself a brandy. At least he knows everything now, Christine thought to herself. What more is there to tell?

'I know you think I'm obsessed with Debra, but believe me, what I have told you is the truth,' she said, trying to hold back the tears. 'I wouldn't make up anything like that. You know I wouldn't. I couldn't, and, Adam, I'm so worried about it all. Typing that e-mail and being mistaken for Debra, then hearing about the baby and . . . '

She stopped speaking as the tears ran unheeded down her cheeks. What more could she say? What more could she do? She watched Adam staring out at the ocean and felt a crying need to feel his arms around her, his voice telling her everything would be all right.

'I can hardly believe you did what you did, so why should I believe you now? Debra's my sister-in-law. I've never given her any cause to think that I could love her or wish to marry her, so what would be the point of her following me?' His voice was granite hard. 'And as for this stupid story

171

about a record card! You're obsessed, Christine, obsessed with jealousy and spite.'

'No, not I'm not. It's all true.'

Panicking now, Christine rained ineffectual blows against his chest. Grabbing hold of her hands, Adam pulled her towards him, brushing away the tears with his fingers as she tried to wrest herself away from him.

'Oh, Christine,' he murmured against her skin. 'Don't be so upset. I had no right to lose control like that.'

'I'm so sorry, Adam, so sorry about the e-mail. Say you forgive me, please! You see, I'm terrified of what Debra might do,' she sobbed. 'Oh, I know it sounds absurd, but what with her and that stupid e-mail, I feel like I've been treading on eggshells.'

'Forget the damned e-mail,' Adam said, drawing her close. 'Forgive you? It's you who should forgive me for causing you so much pain.' He pulled her closer, his arms strong and protective. 'I promise never to act like that again. Well, not without good reason.'

Relieved that the truth was out and that she had not lost Adam's trust, Christine managed a brief smile, and, arms entwined, they wandered over to the veranda, their senses soothed by the sound of the billowing waves.

11

'I've heard from Laura,' Adam said a few days later, as Christine came down to breakfast. 'The festival begins tomorrow and she thinks it best we meet her there. I left it to her to choose a meeting place because she knows her way around and with all the people that are bound to attend, it might be hard for us to find her.'

'Good idea,' Chris said. 'So what did you decide?'

'She suggested we meet outside the Royal Palace. Apparently it's a gingerbread-style building opposite the Catholic church and quite a landmark.'

'Well, I'm sure we'll be able to find it. How do we get there?'

'We fly from Tongatapu. There'll be lots to see and do so I suggest we take it easy today. Lounge on the beach, go for a swim, that sort of thing.'

'We can pick up a picnic at Palola's house.'

Enjoying the sweet scent of the frangipani in the blossom-laden air, they took their time strolling over the footbridge, and were surprised to see Palola lying very still on a frond mattress outside her house.

'Is she all right?' Christine said in an anxious tone. 'She's usually up and about at this time of day, shouting orders to everyone.'

Leaning over Palola's prone body, she shook her gently. The native woman opened her eyes.

'Palola not feeling so good,' she said. 'Cousin had birthday, too much kava. You want picnic?'

'Yes, if you're sure we can't do anything for you,' Christine said.

'Do nothing. I sleep. You go enjoy day. Plenty of food, I think.'

'Now don't you worry about us,' Christine replied. 'We'll pack a hamper and check on you when we come back. Are you sure you'll be all right? You're not in pain, are you?'

'Head in pain. Now you go. Take food, enjoy.'

'She obviously wants to be left alone,' Adam said. 'If she gets any worse, we'll take her to that doctor friend of yours. Well, one of them anyway.'

'I don't know how the islanders can cope with so much kava,' Christine said.

'A couple of glasses does it for me,' Adam replied as they packed a hamper with food and lots of juice. 'I must say I'm looking forward to the festival. Laura will be able to show us the best vantage points. Her brother, David, is due to turn up as well. He sounds a real character, doesn't he?'

After a relaxing day, they made their way back to Palola's house with the empty hamper, and although she was still feeling unwell, Palola refused any help and sent them on their way.

'We'll have to check on her again before we leave for the festival tomorrow,' Adam said, as they spent a blissful evening sitting on the veranda. 'Are you

hungry? Frankly, I couldn't eat a thing.
How about an early night?'

Christine agreed it would be a perfect
end to the day, and happily curled up in
Adam's arms.

'What do you think I should wear?'
was Christine's first question the next
morning. 'It's bound to be hot. Cotton,
I should think, don't you?'

She finally decided on a white cotton
top with matching short-sleeved shirt
and matching skirt.

'We'd better get cracking, hadn't we,
if we want to look in at Palola's?'

Adam had decided to wear a green
T-shirt and matching shorts.

'If you're about ready, we'll be off,'
he said. 'Don't forget your black coral
necklace and bracelet. It will look well
with white.'

Christine put them on and together
they made for Palola's house. She still
wasn't back to her old self, but she
insisted she didn't need any medicine
and told them to go to the festival and
have a good time.

'I hope she doesn't try any of that witch-doctor stuff,' Christine said, looking at the array of pills and potions stuck on a shelf. She'll do herself more harm than good.'

'Well, she managed to look after herself well enough before we came here,' Adam said, 'so perhaps the best thing is for us not to interfere.'

'You're probably right,' Christine said as they walked down the beach to catch the ferry. 'It's just that I can't help worrying about her.'

'Yes, I worry about her, too,' Adam replied, 'but let's make a pact not to worry about anything today. It's the day of the festival, enjoy!'

When they arrived, they had no trouble finding the place Laura had suggested they meet although the streets were very crowded. She gave a cheery wave as soon as she saw them.

'Hi,' she shouted about the noise of a steel band. 'Come over here and take a look at some of these floats. They're out of this world!'

With so much going on, Christine didn't know what to look at first, and, trying to cross over to where Laura was standing meant dodging between the floats and getting caught up in a basket-weaving contest.

'Go on, have a go,' Laura shouted when she saw Christine trying to fight her way through. 'It's easy when you know how.'

Christine laughed and tried her hand at it, but it really was quite difficult for a beginner.

'What about that coconut-husking competition?' she said to Adam, who was soaking up the atmosphere. 'We can't allow you to just stand about. You've got to take part and join in.'

'I don't think that's for me.' Adam laughed. 'I'm just amazed at the variety of decorations, and the costumes, so colourful and co-ordinated. They must have taken months deciding what to wear. And some of those masks — they're bizarre!'

'You're right, they do take months,'

Laura confirmed. 'And the choir on that multi-coloured float has practised for months as well.'

The musical rhythms throbbed through the streets, and the three of them found themselves joining in the dancing, donning either the feathered headdresses or silver sequinned masks and climbing on to one of the floats that was carrying a band.

'Have you seen those wigs some of the girls are wearing?' Christine said. 'They look like long fringes made out of silver paper. Very effective, I think.'

'Yes, they are,' Laura replied. 'And I must tell you, there's a fashion show of traditional Polynesian costumes taking place in a few minutes, like the one at the Tongan Trade Centre. What about you and me taking a look at it while Adam watches the firework display?'

'Yes, lovely,' Christine replied. 'Where do we leave our masks?'

'Oh, just stick them on this float,' Laura said as they climbed down into the street. 'Do you approve of my new hairstyle?' She added as she donned one of the silver wigs for a moment before tossing it away.

Christine was fascinated by the collection of traditional fashion on display and could have stayed there all afternoon, but the girls had promised to meet up with Adam in about an hour's time and together they made their way back to where they'd left him, still taking photographs of the parades.

'I don't know what's happened to David,' Laura remarked, when they met up with Adam. 'I told him exactly where to meet me, but there's no sign of him.' She sighed. 'He does his own thing, goes his own way. Sometimes it's about as easy to get through to him as a granite wall. There's no sign of his girl friend either, but as we've never met, I wouldn't recognise her, would I?'

'Adam, I can't help thinking about Palola,' Christine said. 'She's not at all well, but she insisted that we don't miss the festival. I think I'll leave you with your video camera and make my way back to the island. Is that all right?'

'Yes, of course it is,' Adam replied. 'Laura's anxious to get back, too, in case her brother's gone straight to the plantation. Take care, you two,' he went on, giving Christine a kiss on the cheek.

Christine was glad of Laura's companionship on the return journey, as she'd taken a real liking to the girl. They parted company when they got off the plane, and Christine caught the ferry back to the island.

She hurried along to Palola's house, anxious to make sure the woman was all right. She'd thoroughly enjoyed her day, the carnival atmosphere, the processions, even her poor attempt at basket-weaving, and the fashion show had been gorgeous. In fact, everything had gone her way. She knew that Adam had enjoyed it, too.

Recalling their closeness, her spirits rose. She knew he didn't love her, but maybe loving him as passionately as she did now would more than make up for it. The day had been perfect in every way, and now she could hardly wait for the sultry night to close in when once again she would feel safe and secure in her husband's arms.

Palola was sitting on one of the hammocks, fanning herself with a piece of coconut frond when Christine approached.

'Me better,' she beamed. 'All headache gone.'

'Good,' Christine replied. 'We were worried about leaving you, so I left Adam to his own devices and came back early.'

'You have visitor,' Palola said. 'She say good friend so I let her wait in house. Big surprise, I think.'

Who could it possibly be, Christine thought. Only a few of their friends knew their whereabouts and even if they did, they would hardly be likely to intrude on their privacy.

The door of the fale was ajar. When she went in she saw, sprawling indolently on the settee, a stunningly-attractive dark-haired woman holding a glass in her hand and with a half-bottle of vodka at her feet. Debra! Christine stared at her in disbelief, as a myriad of thoughts raced through her head. What was she doing here? Was she still chasing Adam? How did she know where to find him?

Debra gave Christine one of her tight, little smiles that Christine had come to realise, after that drunken scene at the wedding reception, always came before trouble. Clad in a tight scarlet T-shirt and white shorts, Debra swirled her drink around in her glass.

'Well, if it isn't the blushing bride!' she said. 'I've been waiting for you for hours. Now that Adam's safely out of the way, I think it's time for a little tête-a-tête, don't you? Come in, sit down. Care to join me in a drink?'

Christine hastily gathered her wits together. What on earth was Debra doing here and how did she know about the island?

'Why are you here, Debra?' she stammered out. 'Why are you drinking vodka? You must know it's not good for . . .'

'Not good for what?' Debra queried. 'Just what are you insinuating, Christine?'

'You know very well what I'm talking about,' Christine said in an even tone. 'When I went swimming, I cut my foot on a coral reef. Because I was afraid it might get infected I went to see a doctor in Nuku'alofa.'

Debra shrugged. 'And what has an infected foot got to do with me?'

Christine braced herself before going on.

'Nothing. Just hear me out, will you? I was given a course of antibiotics and went for a check-up later. I saw a different doctor, who asked my name and I told him it was Kyle, but unfortunately his receptionist gave him your medical card in error.'

Debra shrugged again. 'I've the feeling you're playing cat and mouse with me, Christine. What was written on this medical card?'

185

Christine took a deep breath.

'You know very well. Your name, your address at Hunters' Lodge and the fact that you are about six weeks pregnant.'

There I've said it, Christine thought to herself, and gave a sigh of relief.

'As I understand the legal position,' Debra said, uncoiling herself from the settee, 'the relationship between doctor and patient is highly confidential. He'd no right to tell you that. If I reported him he could be struck off the medical register.'

'Believe me, he didn't intend to, and he apologised profusely,' Christine declared firmly. 'I'd seen a lady doctor before but she wasn't on duty that day. The receptionist got mixed up because we are both called Kyle.'

'That doesn't exonerate him. He was careless, very careless.' Debra paused for a moment while she poured herself another drink. 'And you couldn't wait to tell your darling husband, I suppose?'

'Adam knows, yes. After all, you're

part of the family and he's naturally concerned.'

Debra tossed back her hair. 'I bet he is. Where is he now by the way, still at the festival?'

'Yes, I left him. I came back early because I was worried about Palola. She hadn't been feeling too well.'

'Palola? Who's she? Oh, that big native woman who let me in. Your servant.'

'She may look after us, but she's no servant.' Christine felt anger rising in her chest. 'She's our friend.'

Debra remained unimpressed.

'Be that as it may, I'm sure you must be intrigued to know why I'm here.'

'I know you've been following us. You went to the crater and the volcano. The pilot described you to us. You're following Adam, and I don't understand why. How did you find this island?'

'The man at the Visitors' Centre told me how to reach you. You see, I've a special reason for seeing you which I'll tell you about if you'll just sit down for a moment. You're sure you won't have a drink?'

Christine shook her head, and sank down into one of the armchairs.

'For starters, I haven't been following Adam. I've been following David,' Debra said. 'David Hargreaves, that is, Laura Hargreaves' brother. She's stayed here, hasn't she?'

'Yes, but . . . '

'Let me finish. After our visit to the volcano, David managed to elude me. You see, I've got to persuade him the baby I'm expecting is his.'

Christine could hardly believe what she was hearing.

'And it isn't?' she managed to ask.

'I'm not saying it isn't and I'm not saying it is. Truth is, I'm just not one hundred per cent certain. But either way, David's doing everything he can to wriggle out of it. I met this dishy man, you see, the day David and I flew back from New Zealand, and things got a bit out of hand, only David doesn't know about that. And he mustn't ever know. It's important that he thinks he's the father. Now that I've blurted it out, it's got to remain a secret between us, just like your father's grubby little escapades.'

Christine thought her heart would stop. How did Debra know about her father? She couldn't possibly know after all the trouble both she and Adam had taken to keep it confidential. What could she say? She decided to brazen it out.

'I don't know what you're talking about.'

Debra looked down at her tapered fingernails before looking Christine straight in the eye.

'Don't you really? Well, let me jog your memory, Christine. Does the name Jonathan Childes mean anything to you?'

Christine felt as if a knife was twisting in her stomach. Why had Debra mentioned Jonathan Childes? How much did she know? And where had she got her information? Surely not from Childes himself. Her mind in a whirl, Christine fought for control.

'I wondered how you had managed to trap Adam into marriage,' Debra said coyly, 'only I realise now it was the other way round. He knew something, didn't he? Something you were anxious to hide. It was tit-for-tat, wasn't it? You scratch my back and I'll scratch yours.'

'But . . . '

'Oh, I've got copies of all the details. Just give me a minute and I'll show you.'

Debra rummaged in her handbag and Christine recognised a copy of the contract signed by Jonathan Childes.

'This is a copy, of course,' she continued, thrusting the document under Christine's nose. 'The original's still locked in the bureau at Hunters' Lodge.'

Christine couldn't believe the evidence of her own eyes. Why had Debra done this? What did she hope to gain by it?

'Yes, I recognise it,' she said quietly. 'I left the original locked in the bureau. How did you get the key?'

'Adam gave it to me, of course,' Debra told her mockingly. 'I didn't bother looking in the bureau at first, then I thought there might be something valuable in it.' She laughed her high-pitched laugh. 'But until I opened it, I didn't realise just how valuable.'

'But he couldn't! He wouldn't have given you the key.'

Christine tried to reject the impact Debra's words were having on her state of mind.

'He knew the importance of keeping this matter strictly confidential.'

'Anyone with half an eye would realise that,' Debra said, 'but that didn't stop him from handing over the key. I realise now why he wanted to marry you. It wasn't because he fell in love with you. Oh, no. He may not love me but he certainly doesn't love you. The only mistress or love Adam has ever had is his work. Always has been and always will be. And there's another thing. He didn't marry you just to get control of your father's company. Why should a corporate assassin like Adam want to bother with a tin-pot antiques firm? Oh, I reckon he'll make a bob or two now he's turned the company around, but it's not the money, it's the challenge that counts. He can't resist a challenge. But quite apart from that, he married you to rid himself of all his unwanted female admirers, killing two birds with one stone. Like flies round a honeypot, they were, and he hated it. Would do anything to get them off his back.'

Snatching back the copy contract, Debra waved it in the air.

'So what's this worth, Christine? What are you willing to pay for me to keep quiet?'

For a moment or two, Christine didn't say a thing, as Debra's words echoed round and round in her head. She was burning all over, rage, humiliation and fear rendering her speechless. If Debra was speaking the truth, Adam had betrayed her. That in itself was bad enough. But how could she possibly negotiate with Debra? Her future prospects as Adam's wife didn't bear thinking about, but she knew if she was to keep her confidence and self-respect she mustn't let Debra's allegations wear her down.

'Tell me the truth, Debra,' she said. 'You don't really want David, do you? But you'll let him act as a stop-gap rather than be left to cope on your own with a baby whose father you're not sure of. What you really want is for Adam to leave me, in the forlorn hope that eventually he'll marry you so the baby can be adopted as his own.'

'Yes, spot on. You catch on quickly, Christine,' Debra said in a gleeful tone. 'That's exactly what I want. David would only be second best. I've always wanted Adam, and he knows it. Trouble is, he won't do anything about it, but things are different now. I've waited and played the long game, and now he's mine!'

'And what makes you think I can persuade Adam to do what you want?'

'To keep your father's name out of the tabloids. I've already told you Adam's married to his job. It wouldn't look good, would it, to read about an entrepreneur's wife in a fraud scandal. If the gutter Press got hold of it, and the media, his future, his credibility and his professional reputation would all be potentially at great risk. Come on, Christine, it wouldn't be such a sacrifice would it?' Debra went on. 'Don't kid yourself Adam really loves you. If he did, he wouldn't let you wear that rubbishy black coral jewellery. He'd insist on giving you black pearls, the real thing.'

Christine needed time to think and Debra's jibes were getting on her nerves.

'I don't want to hear any more of this,' her furious reply came as she flung the door wide open. 'Please, get out of here.'

Debra stuffed the copy contract in her bag and moved towards the door.

'I'll give you twenty-four hours to decide what you're going to do,' she said, glancing at her watch. 'That Palola person told me what time I could pick up the ferry, so I might as well be on my way.'

When she reached the wooden bridge, she stopped to have a final word.

'I'm staying at the International Hotel in Nuku'alofa,' she shouted, 'so you can contact me there. I wouldn't take too long about it either if I were in your shoes. Be seeing you.'

12

Still in shock, Christine ran up the stairs and started to pack an overnight bag, misery clenching inside her like a fist. She couldn't stay here, not after Debra's revelations. She'd trusted Adam and he'd betrayed her. She had to get away.

Why had he given Debra the bureau key? Whatever had possessed him? He must have known Debra's curiosity would get the better of her, and now the effect of that would reflect not only on Christine herself but on him as well, unless Debra could be persuaded to keep quiet, and there seemed little likelihood of that. Christine shut the lid of her bag. Perhaps Adam hadn't given her the key. But who else could have done so? Even as she tried to find excuses for him, the cold fingers of doubt were growing, spreading, tainting their newly-idyllic relationship.

Where could she go? That was the question now. She didn't want to go to Nuku'alofa with Debra still swanning around. The nearest place she could think of was the Hargreaves' banana plantation. The island was only a hop away and Laura was bound to let her stay overnight. Having made her decision, she told Palola she was going away for the night and hitched a lift on a cargo vessel that was taking supplies to the Hargreaves' island.

Laura was at the pier, clip-board in hand, awaiting the boat and checking off the goods.

'Don't let me disturb you,' Christine said. 'Is it all right if I go up to the house?'

'Of course,' Laura replied. 'I didn't think I'd see you again so soon. David hasn't contacted me and Dad's working on the other side of the plantation. Go in, and help yourself to a drink. I won't be long.'

Once inside the house, Christine

paced up and down until Laura arrived.

'Christine,' Laura said, as soon as she walked into the house, 'you look dreadful. Have you been crying? Whatever's the matter?'

'It's Adam, or rather it's something his sister-in-law's just told me about him. I can't go into it, Laura. I hope you understand, but I just had to get away. Will it be all right if I stay overnight?'

'Of course, it will,' Laura replied, putting her arm round Christine's shoulder, and giving her a hug. 'Don't worry. I won't ask you any more about it. But I must say I'm surprised if something's gone wrong between you and Adam. You look so lovey-dovey when you're together. I thought you two were joined at the hip.'

Christine managed a brief smile.

'So did I until this trouble cropped up. My face is all streaked, isn't it? Can I use your bathroom and clean myself up?'

'Yes, it's upstairs on the right. Don't

hurry. I'll make some strong coffee when you come down.'

Having washed her face, Christine walked into the nearest bedroom and lay down on the bed. Closing her eyes, she tried to pretend none of this was happening to her, that it was all some dreadful nightmare from which she would soon awaken. She'd no idea she'd fallen asleep until she heard voices coming from downstairs — Laura's voice and a man's voice, which she instantly recognised as Adam's. Next minute he had bolted up the stairs and was standing over her. Christine cringed away from him, mentally bracing herself.

'How could you?' she said hotly. 'You're despicable. You've broken my heart. How did you know I was here? Just leave me alone.'

'Laura rang me on my mobile saying you were very distressed. You seemed very happy at the festival. What's happened? Tell me. I demand to know.'

'Just get away from me,' Christine

said shakily. 'I'm sick and tired of being threatened by you and your family. I still can't believe what you've done.'

'What have I done? Christine, please. I can't bear to see you like this. Tell me, please.'

'When I got back to the island, Debra was waiting for me and . . . '

'Debra? I'll kill her if she's been causing trouble. What did she say?'

'It isn't only what she said, even though that was bad enough. She brought a copy of the contract that Jonathan Childes had signed. She knew all about my father and started making threats.'

'But you locked all the confidential documents in the bureau at Hunters' Lodge.'

'Don't you think I know that? It's all your fault. She told me you'd given her the key.'

'And you believed her? Oh, my poor Christine. No wonder you're in such a state. I didn't give her the key, I swear. Why should I do such a thing? There must be some other explanation, and I'll not rest until I know the truth. Where's Debra now? Still on the island?'

Feeling Adam's arms close around her, she breathed a sigh of relief. It was clear he wasn't lying, but in order to make things right between them, he'd have to get to the bottom of this.

'She's staying at the International Hotel in Nuku'alofa. She told me I'd got twenty-four hours to get you to agree to leave me and end the marriage.'

'She said what? She must be out of her mind. What did she threaten you with?'

'Going to the media about my father. She made the same threats you did before we were married.'

'But not for the same reason, I assure you. What else did she say?'

'She was jealous of me because I married you. She said the baby she was expecting, which we all thought might be David's, probably wasn't his at all, because she'd had a one-night stand and David didn't know about it. She wants you to divorce me and eventually marry her so you will adopt the child and . . . Oh, I can't tell you any more, it's too painful.'

'Come back with me, my darling Christine. Leave Debra to me. If you'll just wait for me on the island where we've been so happy together, everything will become clear to you.'

'But what about Laura?'

'I'll tell Laura you're going back with me. Only trust me, that's all I ask. What I have to tell you, can't be said here and now. It will have to wait until we get back. Just hold this one thought in your mind, Christine, that I didn't give Debra that key. Please, Christine, believe me, please. I'm going to find Debra now and put paid to all this nonsense.'

Christine didn't know how she got through the next few hours back on their island as she waited for Adam to return from his meeting with Debra.

How could she have doubted him? she chided herself. How could I have fallen in love with someone I couldn't trust? When he returns, I must ask him to forgive me.

When she eventually heard him cross the wooden bridge, she ran out to meet him, anxious to hear what he had to say.

'There's no need to worry about Debra any more,' he said. 'I was wrong when I said she was no threat, but I've given her a dose of her own medicine. If she discloses one word about your father, I have threatened to tell David that the baby she is expecting may not be his. Then she'll have nobody to turn to, except me, and I will disown her. She's very vulnerable at the moment, despite her scurrilous tactics, and she won't be bothering either of us again if she wants to remain part of the family.'

'But how did she get the key?'

'Well, it wasn't on the bunch of keys the housekeeper handed over, but Debra was intrigued when she saw the bureau and couldn't find a key to fit it. She called in a firm of locksmiths and they managed to pick the lock. When she opened the bureau and found she had some ammunition, the temptation to try and split us up just proved too much.'

Christine's spirits rose. All was right with her world again.

'I should never have doubted you, Adam. Will you ever forgive me? It was so difficult to imagine how Debra could have got hold of the key if she didn't get it from you, and she sounded so convincing.'

Adam cradled her in his arms.

'There's nothing to forgive. The original contract is still locked away and Debra has given me the only key that fits.' He smiled. 'Now let's forget about her. There's something I've got to tell you, something much more important to both of us.' He gave her hand a squeeze. 'I know you think this started out as an arranged marriage, but I never at any time intended it to be less than a real marriage.'

Christine stared at him, wondering what he was going to say next.

'If you remember, I gave you valid reasons for wanting to marry you, but they were only partly true.'

'I can't think clearly when you're near me,' Christine said. 'I don't know what you mean.'

'When your father brought me back to Hunters' Lodge that first night, do you remember that?'

Christine nodded.

'Well, something happened to me that I wouldn't have dreamed possible. I met you and almost instantly I fell in love. I knew you despised me. You didn't even like me. You told me as much when I asked you to marry me. How would you have reacted if I told you I had fallen in love with you, that I would have given anything, done anything, to make you my wife? You would have shunned me even more. I had to make excuses then, but I'm not making excuses now. I love you. I always have.'

Christine saw the need in his eyes, the leap of desire so hot that she trembled in his arms.

'And I love you,' she said. 'It's true I hated you at first, but I have grown to love you despite everything. Love, the word feels like nectar in my mouth. I've learned to love everything about you. Don't you realise that?'

'And the island,' Adam said. 'Would you still love me if the island was developed?'

Christine didn't hesitate. 'Yes, I'd still love you,' she said. 'That's the trouble with love. It doesn't give you any choice. And if it's your choice to . . . '

'No. You can breathe freely again,' Adam told her with a smile. 'I've given it a lot of thought, and now that I've come to know Palola and the islanders, and listened to what you've had to say, I've decided to leave the island exactly as it is. It's paradise. And now that we've found a place in paradise, we must make sure we keep a place in each other's hearts. There are magical moments waiting for us,' he said. 'Everything else has just slipped into the background and there's only you left.'

'The Kingdom of Tonga is known as the land where time begins,' Christine told him, slipping her hand in his. 'And time is just beginning for us.'

THE END

We do hope that you have enjoyed reading this large print book.

Did you know that all of our titles are available for purchase?

We publish a wide range of high quality large print books including:
Romances, Mysteries, Classics
General Fiction
Non Fiction and Westerns

Special interest titles available in large print are:
The Little Oxford Dictionary
Music Book, Song Book
Hymn Book, Service Book

Also available from us courtesy of Oxford University Press:
Young Readers' Dictionary
(large print edition)
Young Readers' Thesaurus
(large print edition)

For further information or a free brochure, please contact us at:
Ulverscroft Large Print Books Ltd.,
The Green, Bradgate Road, Anstey,
Leicester, LE7 7FU, England.
Tel: (00 44) **0116 236 4325**
Fax: (00 44) **0116 234 0205**

Other titles in the
Linford Romance Library:

FAITHFUL TO A DREAM

Sheila Holroyd

Menna Williams is a talented woman, determined to make her own way in a male-dominated world. When she becomes housekeeper at Bryn Hyfryd, Menna has grander dreams in mind and, with the help of the dashing Tal Lloyd, it seems they will become reality. But Tal's younger brother, Rhodri, is constantly warning Menna about Tal's reckless nature. Gwennan Lloyd, mistress of Bryn Hyfryd, has problems of her own to overcome. Which of her two nephews, Tal or Rhodri, should she trust?

LOVE'S LOST TREASURE

Joyce Johnson

When Rosie Treloar discovers her fiancé is an unscrupulous conman, she flees London for her native Cornwall. Here, she takes a job as a tourist guide and meets American Ben Goodman, who is researching the mystery of his family's legacy, lost during the English civil war. Rosie, increasingly attracted to Ben, becomes involved with his mission, unaware that there are other sinister forces seeking the legacy — forces which could threaten her new found happiness with Ben . . .